ıcy

FRED

An Adult Parable by Jacqueline L. Clarke

MATOU Communications
Copyright 1999 © by Jacqueline L. Clarke
Published by MATOU Communications
3153-M Anchorway Court
Falls Church, VA 22042
Phone and Fax 703 207-3574
ISBN 0-9660596-2-X
Library of Congress Catalog Card No. 99-095672

There's no such thing as an original idea. Everything in this book is a product of the wisdom of others. I take no credit for these thoughts which might be considered plagiarism if I knew their source. Consequently, I've attributed them to my cats.

This book is dedicated to those who've shared their experience, strength and hope with me, the cats who've shared their unconditional love with me, my family whose shared their enthusiasm for these books with me, and, most of all, you readers who have shared your thoughts with me and made it all worthwhile.

Other books by Jacqueline L. Clarke: NATHAN, The Spiritual Journey of an Uncommon Cat, printed 1997, 1998

Nathan, Spiritual Advisor
to BILL and BOB, printed 1998.

Illustrations by Charles H. Clarke

ISBN No.0-9660596-2-X
Library of Congress Catalog Card Number 99-095672

To order additional copies of this book or Jackie Clarke's other books, see **page 121 in the back of this book.**

Forward

This is the last book in the Nathan Trilogy, which began with the 1997 publication of *NATHAN...The Spiritual Journey of an Uncommon Cat*. What was originally intended as a heartfelt tribute to a creature who provided me with unconditional love for eighteen years, soon turned into something quite different as Nathan assumed my personality and began learning the "life" lessons to which I was becoming privy in my quest for happiness. Through a magical transformation, Nathan developed the same moral values, social skills, and deeper understanding of spirituality that I was experiencing. However, Nathan only had one teacher, a rabbit incarcerated across the street for sex offenses; while my teachers were many— and from all walks of life.

In the second book, *Nathan, Spiritual Advisor to Bill and Bob*, Bob recounts more humorous observations on life and spirituality which he's learned from Nathan. In this third book, *Nathan's Spiritual Legacy, Fred*, Fred documents new lessons he's learned from both Nathan and Bob — the same insights I've gained since writing the previous books.

When I started this project, I chose humor as the vehicle to deliver practical messages about life's common problems and the search for spirituality because much of what I learned was learned through laughter. If there's one thing upon which I absolutely insist, it is enjoying life! It is my fervent hope that you receive as much enjoyment reading the Nathan Trilogy as I experienced writing it.

Table of Contents

Nathan's Introduction

It's another glorious morning with the sun streaming through the curtains covering the picture window in the living room. The house is still and the neighborhood is completely quiet. It's too early for the sounds of thudding cans and tinkling bottles tossed into the recesses of yawning garbage trucks ... too early for the revving of automobile engines by anxious commuters trying to win the "Washington 500" race to work by shaving a few seconds off their best time ... too early for the cawing of big, ugly crows — winged rats — picking through plastic ... too early for the barking of dogs, out for their morning bowel movements. (Thank God, I don't have to hold back the forces of nature until a human is ready and willing to take me for "a walk" — a euphemism for depositing the contents of one's intestines on someone else's property with the rationalization that they are bio-degradable.)

As the oldest and wisest Clarke cat, I am so grateful for everything I have today — the quiet mornings; the comfortable bed and "Posturepedic" mattress I share with my human, The Won (short for *The Hairless **Won**der); my cozy house with its magnificent view of the entire *cul-de-sac;* my lush, tree-shaded yard, protected by my pungent scent and adequate fencing; my three square meals a day of fish and shrimp cassoulet; The Won himself; and the adopted brothers with whom I reside.

In order of seniority, my siblings include: Angus, The Cute, a white and blonde Himalayan, not the sharpest tool in the drawer, but very personable; Bill and Bob, two wombmates

----

*"Hairless" refers to The Won's lack of fur rather than follicles.

1

who finally transcended awkward adolescence to achieve a certain nobility, well-camouflaged by their "Laurel and Hardy" appearance; and Fred, an arrogant little "tough," who's a black and white tuxedo kitten and the newest addition to the family.

Like myself and Bob, Fred was born restless, irritable and discontented, doomed to a life of lonely self-reliance until he became willing to change. I changed by putting into practice essential "life lessons" that I learned from my mentor, **BR**, short for **B**unny **R**abbit, who was incarcerated across the street for sex offenses (until his death from obesity, which he insisted was a result of being over-served). I hadn't meant to change and grow; I only wanted a captive audience to listen to my troubles. BR, well-endowed in the ear department, proved to be a great listener who evolved into an exceptional teacher as soon as the student (me — Nathan) was ready. BR guided me through a personality conversion that led me from seeing life as a problem to be solved,to viewing it as a journey to be enjoyed.

While I struggled to hold on to each of my nine lives, which were slipping away as a result of my self-will run riot, BR taught me such practical lessons as: Happiness isn't having what you want, but wanting what you have. Plan but don't project — take positive action rather than anticipating negative results. Honesty is complete harmony of thought, word and deed. Resentments are like taking poison and waiting for your opponent to die. Keep your head where your feet are planted and only talk to those who are present; and life's greatest achievement is surviving a difficult fate with dignity and courage, then teaching others how to do the same.

But the greatest gift I received from BR was my spirituality — the relationship I developed with a Nathan-friendly supreme being who loves me unconditionally and guides my life accordingly. Spooked by the thought of religion, I was sure spirituality was the same thing until BR explained that they were quite different. He said religion consisted of rules and rituals made by others to honor God; while spirituality was my own personal relationship with God which had no rules, save one — the Golden Rule. Furthermore, spirituality wasn't a belief; it was a feeling — of peace and love expressed through helping others. It was about being useful and whole, not holy.

Under BR's direction, I learned how to be happy, and I cataloged all the "life lessons" he taught me in my journal, *NATHAN... The Spiritual Journey of an Uncommon Cat*. I had to refer to this journal frequently when it was my turn to become a mentor to Bill and Bob, two new kittens who moved into the household.

Bob, who was as arrogant and defensive as I was at his age, required the most work but, like a sponge, he absorbed practical lessons like: Life is only 10% what you make it and 90% how you take it. When you're going through Hell, keep moving. Happiness is wanting what you have and believing it is enough. Life is what happens while you're busy making other plans. The difference between a demand and a request is your willingness to accept "no" for an answer. Anger is a poison that eats its own container; and meaningful self-improvement for the long term is seldom accomplished in the short term.

In addition to learning these lessons, Bob was guided to his own belief in a loving God or Higher Meower, who has only one of three answers for anything he asks today — yes, later, or I have something better planned for you. Bob firmly believes that who we are is God's gift to us, but what we become is our gift to Him, and he's cataloged everything he's learned in his journal, *Nathan, Spiritual Advisor to Bill and Bob*, in which he was kind enough to give me top billing.

When Bob rescued Fred and brought him to live with us, I assumed Bob would become Fred's mentor, guiding him through the process that would turn his defiance and self-reliance into serenity and trust. But I was wrong. Initially there was no chemistry between Bob and Fred, who arched his back and spit every time Bob offered him a suggestion. So the task of mentor once again fell to me. Today, however, both Bob and I are leading Fred on the path to spirituality and its ultimate promise, The Vision, the ability to understand and accept God's will — even if only in hindsight — and feel a deep sense of allegiance with Him that makes everything all right.

I explained to Fred that the journey he was on couldn't be accomplished overnight and that, although there would be plenty of rewards along the way, it would probably be years before he acquired The Vision, a concept that was much too advanced for Fred right now. He listened patiently while batting a real-fur mouse around, and his only question was, "When can I have a girlfriend?"

Not everyone who finds spirituality attains The Vision, but I know Fred will, in time, as soon as he gets his priorities in order. I suggested that Fred keep a journal, just as Bob and I have. He promised he would and has been true to his word — because what follows is Fred's account of his journey...my spiritual legacy.

Nathan — January, 1999

4

Chapter One
Fred's Story

As soon as I heard The Won open the sliding glass door to the deck, I hurdled over Angus on the landing, raced down the stairs, and jumped over the prone forms of Billy and Bobby. I dodged Nathan, who was rounding the corner from the kitchen, just in time to see The Won spit a peach pit out the open door, over the deck, and onto the lawn. I was nearly outside when I suddenly found myself clamped vice-like between the door and the metal jam. I emitted an ear-splitting meow that nearly caused The Won to choke on the rest of his peach as he quickly slid the door open again to release me. (The Won might be getting old, but he still had lightening-fast reflexes from years of accidentally stepping on Nathan's tail.)

"Damn it, Fred, you're going to get yourself killed some day if you're not more careful," he said, bending to pat me down and assure himself that I had no broken ribs.

I was often guilty of disregarding my own safety in the rush to get where I was going — the same way The Won always tried to beat traffic lights that were about to turn red by racing underneath them. I meowed pitifully when The Won put me in the car for a visit to the vet. Although The Won assumed I was afraid of the vet, what really terrified me was his aggressive driving. It was clear we were both A-type personalities, undoubtedly the reason we were so *simpatico*.

Aggressive driving had become a real problem in the Washington area, now distinguished for having the second worst traffic congestion in the United States — second only to Los Angeles where cars sported bumper stickers that read, "Cover me, I'm changing lanes." I knew enough to lay low for awhile after The Won returned from driving anywhere because he was always in such a foul mood. He had a bumper sticker that read "Honk if you want to see my finger," but he had sense enough to leave it home because he was often as guilty of being a "honker" as a "honkee." (I knew the term "honkee" was coined in Los Angeles; now I understood its origin.)

Like The Won, I was impatient and always in a hurry, even though there was never any reason to be. (The only factors that influenced my schedule were mealtimes and 10 p.m., when The Won called me in for the night.) So I had no excuse for my behavior, except that I lived in Washington where a display of urgency made whatever you were doing seem more important. I also succumbed to another Washington affectation — the less available you were, the more in demand you seemed. So I'd occasionally hide from The Won, forcing him to scour the neighborhood calling my name, which created an illusion of popularity and made me seem in great demand.

I was much closer to The Won than to any of my siblings because he was more tolerant of my behavior. When I erred by doing something I shouldn't — or conversely, by not doing something I should — The Won forgave me as soon as I rolled over on my back to apologize. My brothers, on the other hand, were not as susceptible to my charms. When I misbehaved, they expected me to make amends by changing my behavior, not merely apologizing for it.

I loved The Won and tried my best to please him, but sometimes there was no pleasing humans who, I was

6

convinced, suffered from neurotic ambivalence. When I was inside, The Won wanted me outside, and when I was outside, he wanted me inside where I insisted on being close to him — so close, I stayed right under his feet where he could easily find me (and often did, by tripping over me in the dark, on the stairs, or with his arms full of groceries). When I wasn't at his feet, I was literally in his face, inserting myself between him and his newspaper or lying right across the pages of whatever book he was reading. But no matter where we were, no sooner would I get settled in than he would invite me out again.

Some considered me "tough," but I liked to think of myself as resilient, a direct result of surviving my youth. When I was only a kitten, I was prematurely forced to leave my family because of a vicious "tom" named Tiger my Momcat invited to live with us to protect us. But Tiger was insanely jealous of me, the only male in the family, and started beating me. So when it was just "he and me," Fred bled; it was that simple.

I wasn't afraid for myself — that wasn't why I left. I was terrified that Tiger's jealous rage would spill over from me to my Momcat and three sisters, a wholesome black and white who resembled me and two delicate dark blondes. Since I was the source of Tiger's rage, I thought his belligerence would leave when I did. So I became a reluctant, scared, and ill-prepared "knight of the open road."

I lived on the streets for months, foraging from dumpsters and plastic trash bags, until I found the regular supply of food The Won left at the top of his hill for the racoons. I looked pretty pathetic by then, which is when Bobby discovered me. I was barely alive by the time he "rescued" me because it took him a week to decide to bring me home to The

7

Won. I didn't resent him for waiting so long before doing the right thing because, I admit, I was a sorry-looking sight and lacked the most rudimentary social skills, which he undoubtedly intuited.

I hadn't been exposed to members of my own species other than my immediate family, which was all female except for Tiger, the evil tom. I should have been terrified by an entire household of tomcats — and one human, a species with which I had no experience — but I was too sick to care. Quite frankly, I didn't have the energy to be frightened and, by the time I got well, there was no reason to be. By then, I knew I'd lucked into a relatively peaceful port where I could weather life's storms.

Recognizing that The Won was the seat of power, I figuratively remained in his lap rather than bonding with my own species. I definitely didn't like Bobby, who acted like he "owned" me just because he was the one who brought me here. (If there's one thing I resent, it's authority figures telling me what I *must* do, a syndrome I call "must-erbation.") So I avoided Bobby at all costs and the others on general principle. I put all my emotional eggs in The Won's basket; consequently, when he became ill and unavailable, I was lost. Sure my luck was taking its usual turn for the worse, I began acting out.

Nathan was the one who saw how troubled I was and who called me on my behavior. He assured me I'd always have a home with him and the others and that I'd never have to be alone again, no matter what happened to The Won. He told me we were a family, and families stuck together in good times and in bad. I didn't want to end up living and dying on the streets, so I decided to trust Nathan, who told me to trust a higher power instead, adding that neither he nor The Won were It. (I thought it was mandatory for anyone Nathan's age to be wise and truthful. Little did I know he wasn't *that* old; actually, he'd probably never live to be as old as he looked.)

Nathan encouraged me to find a user-friendly God or Higher Meower, a universal source of goodness and love. Nathan insisted he wasn't trying to convince me of the *existence of God, only the need for one of my own understanding.* Because I wanted to please him, I agreed to compromise my agnosticism and join Bobby and him in the den every day for prayer and meditation, even though I didn't know to whom I was praying and didn't have a clue as to how to meditate.

So the three of us began meeting every afternoon in the den under a picture of Nathan and BR, where I initially confused meditation with daydreaming — when I managed to stay awake at all. Nathan was patient, convinced that my mind would eventually get lonesome enough to join my body. He said it was essential that I eventually believe, but the only thing I really needed to believe right now was that everything was going to be all right. And I did.

Darting out the back door, across the patio, and into the tall grass, I watched The Won watching me. I'd learned that it was as impossible to have a bad day with a good attitude as it was to have a good day with a bad attitude; so I always started out on a positive note. When I felt overwhelmed by life, I'd try to remember Nathan's "one day at a time" slogan and put it into practice. However, sometimes several days conspired to attack me at once. Yesterday was a good example.

9

No sooner had I come out, than a bird flying overhead dumped on me. "They sing for some creatures," I thought in disgust. And no sooner had I finished licking myself clean from that affront than an egg from a nest in the tree I was climbing slimed me. When I cleaned myself up for a second time and went into the front yard for a nap in the sun, I was rudely awakened by the barking of the dog next door. By then, I was so irritated, I had a chip on my shoulder the size of a redwood.

I gave up trying to nap outside and went into the house, looking forward to resuming my snooze in my favorite chair, but Bob and Bill were already in it, curled up and sleeping. Now I was really pissed...and had a litany of reasons to be!

"Where are you going, Fred?" Nathan asked, as I marched by him on my way to the bedroom.

Nathan was the last person I wanted to talk to, but before I knew it, I was disgorging the furball of emotions that seethed within me. Although I didn't intend to make myself feel better, I did, as soon as I vented my anger. Nathan always said feelings weren't right or wrong, they just were — and he never discounted or belittled mine. However, that didn't stop him from sharing his thoughts with me.

"Hmm," Nathan mused. "It isn't even noon and you've already racked up four resentments when nothing that's happened to you today was really about you at all! I doubt that bird was aiming for you, Fred. That was just an accident. As for the egg, what a pity some mother bird tragically lost one of her young. And the dog — he was probably barking because he was lonely, hungry or both... not as lucky as you, able to come in and out of the house and eat whenever you like. As for your chair, you're lucky you have one. Some owners don't even allow pets on their furniture! Sounds to me like you need an attitude adjustment, my friend!"

I flushed with embarrassment, feeling mildly chastised. I knew better than to let life affect my attitude instead of making my attitude affect my life. I was being self-centered instead of grateful for everything I had, which included the option to start my day over at any time. So instead of adding Nathan to my list of resentments, I made a decision to enjoy the rest of the day and went back outside.

Just as I stepped off the deck, however, another bird flew overhead pelting me with its waste. I felt like Bill Murray in the movie *Groundhog Day,* where he kept re-living the same day over and over again. Perhaps I should start my day over — *inside,* I thought, hastily retreating back through my cat door.

The Won was at the dining room table with a pile of papers spread out before him. I jumped to the chair, then to the table, stretching out in a patch of morning sunshine. I'd seen Angus do this a hundred times and thought I'd keep The Won company, just like Angus did.

The Won patted me on the head, just like he patted Angus. When he resumed what he was doing, I closed my eyes to nap but was distracted by the sound of his pen scratching on paper. Slowly opening one eye, I observed the movement of the pen — up, down, and around it went in small circles. Then, just as The Won completed a large looping motion, I couldn't stop myself — my paw darted out and slapped that pen silly, causing it to skid across the paper.

"Damn it, Fred. Look what you made me do!" The Won hollered, tearing up the check he'd been writing. I was miffed by his reprimand and my family allegiance shifted accordingly. When I complained to Nathan about The Won's ill humor, Nathan said that wasn't about me either. The Won was often in a foul mood when he had to deal with finances. Despite being "well-heeled," The Won felt less financially secure, and consequently more resentful about paying bills, the older he got. The process of writing checks was so painful for The Won, Nathan equated it to having his money surgically removed.

Being around all these mood-altering creatures was affecting my serenity adversely, so I did the most sensible thing I could think of at the time — I went to bed.

The next morning, I awoke with an emotional hangover and little joy in my heart. I hadn't even left the bed yet, and I was already irritated. Trotting down to the living room, I looked around the house thinking: "same ol', same ol', same ol' stuff — a few ratty real-fur mice; a feather on a stick or two; Angus, underneath the dining room table, sucking up to The Won for attention; Nathan, still in bed; and Bill and Bob, chasing each other." (Their play was generally harmless, but every once in awhile Billy would demonstrate a cruel streak by taking a real swipe at Bobby and giving him a fat eye.)

Was this really what my life had come to? "Is this all there is?" I asked myself. Where was the excitement? Nathan and Bobby kept harping on me about serenity, but serenity must be an acquired taste, I thought, because it sounded really boring. I knew if I hung around the house, I'd only feel worse; so I went outside to find a playmate. I spotted the mother bird whose egg had slimed me and from whom I was 100% ready to accept an apology. I crept up to the base of the tree in which she was sitting (old habits die hard) and started chattering at her. She seemed interested and I was sure she'd eventually come down, but, like instant gratification, it was taking too long — so I left.

Angus' favorite squirrel was busy burying a nut next to the deck. Remembering what Nathan said about being of use to others, I sauntered over to offer my services, but he bolted up a tree when he saw me coming. So I climbed to the second level of the yard to visit the mole instead. I reached into his hole as far as I could, but he didn't appear to be home. "Bummer!" I thought.

When I talked to Bobby about my lack of success finding a playmate, he told me he wasn't surprised. While I had only the best of intentions, the bird, the squirrel and the mole weren't judging me by my intentions. They were judging me by my previous actions, which had basically terrorized them.

Bobby said I should stick to my own kind. I was trying too hard to be unique, and, at this stage of my development, being a "nonconformist" wasn't healthy for me. Instead, I needed to learn how to be a creature among creatures. I needed a firm foundation in tradition and values before I even considered trying out any original thinking. So he suggested I concentrate on becoming better friends with Angus and Billy before I went out into the world proffering the paw of friendship to every other species.

"Bummer," I thought.

Chapter Two
Defiance and Compliance

My favorite time of day was night, when darkness descended over our cozy *cul-de-sac*. I silently blessed the architect who designed the neighborhood houses to include floor-to-ceiling front picture windows, because there was nothing I enjoyed more than being a "peeping tom." Cruising from one decorative planter to another, nose pressed to the bottom window pane, I loved observing typical American families: Dad, asleep in his big armchair in front of a flickering TV; one and a half children, sprawled on the floor fighting with one another; and the portly family dog, who's only exercise these days was shedding. The missing link, Mom, was either in the kitchen doing what Moms do in kitchens or out at a meeting being socially or personally responsible.

Even though I was thoroughly engrossed in what I was doing, my ear automatically cocked when I heard the sound of my name. I looked inside at the clock on our neighbor's fireplace mantle, confirming that it was 10 p.m. The Won was so punctual, I could set my watch by him— if I had one, that is.

"Fred, Fred, it's 10 p.m. I know you're out there and you can hear me," The Won called. "It's time to come in, Fred." The Won worked hard at sounding respectful, yet authoritative, but I still resented the fact that I was expected to drop everything and "come" when I was called. Dogs come when they are called; cats take a message and get back to you. Didn't he understand? I chafed. Besides, I wasn't ready to go home yet. My job wasn't done.

"So many houses, so little time," I thought. I still had five more houses to visit on this block. Even then, I was sure I would miss something if I obeyed The Won's call to quarters. (Bobby said I was afflicted at birth with FMS, "Fear of Missing Something," and he was right.)

I listened to The Won, who'd come outside twice more to call my name, while I wrestled with my conscience. If I opted to stay out all night (which I frequently did), I'd have to endure "the walk of shame" up the front stairs in the morning. Feeling like a degenerate, I'd be greeted by the accusatory stares of my peers and The Won.

I knew the "morning after" drill by heart. Unfortunately, I'd used up the ration of goodwill to which I was entitled as a newcomer. Now The Won tried to make me feel guilty, telling me how disappointed he was in my behavior before putting me under house arrest to teach me a lesson. Exhausted from my night out, I'd actually welcome the opportunity to sleep for the first few hours of my incarceration, but when I awoke, I'd rail at the injustice of my punishment.

Nathan would inevitably ask me if my night out had been worth it, and I would always insist that it had, whether I believed it or not. Usually I wasn't lying, however, thanks to my penchant for euphoric recall where travel was concerned. My adventures were always more exciting and interesting in retrospect than when I was actually experiencing them. So how could I be accused of lying, when half the time I didn't know what the truth was?

I remembered when no one cared where I was — when I was forced to steal to keep body and soul together. I was

15

incapable of forming a true partnership with another creature — the high cost of my low living. In those days I loved no one, was indifferent to most, and disliked the many. I was isolated, alone, afraid and unhappy, although I didn't always know it. Occasionally I confused feeling good with being happy, not understanding that the former was physical while the latter was emotional. However, even being happy stopped far short of the joy (the ultimate spiritual "high") I had yet to experience.

I really am in a much better place today, I consoled myself, despite not being perfect. If only I could get over my attitude that the house rules didn't apply to me, I'd improve my life immeasurably, I knew. However, I was stubborn, particularly about the 10 p.m. curfew which hit me where I lived. What I treasured most was my freedom to come and go as I pleased, and why not? It was what I did best. So as soon as someone took away that right and I lost my wiggle room, I felt trapped and went nuts.

Much to their credit, Nathan and Bobby were more patient with me than I would have been in similar circumstances. They understood my rebellion, and even tolerated my insistence on always having the last word in an argument — for awhile. Then Nathan asked me to remove "yea but, you don't understand" and "I know" from my vocabulary. He was a crafty old tom because once I did, I had little to say — until I started answering his rhetorical questions with "I don't know." This left him speechless because it was impossible to argue with "I don't know."

Into my second morning of punishment, I was literally throwing myself bodily against the glass patio door to protest my confinement. I'd developed a bad case of the "Yikes,"

16

projecting that my house arrest would be interminable. I was jumping out of my skin, panicked by uncertainty, until Bobby came to tell me that I'd served my sentence and could go out in the yard under his supervision.

"Nathan wants me to show you which plants are edible in case you ever get lost," Bobby said in a matter-of-fact tone. "Some plants are poisonous and you'll get sick if you eat them. Grass is always OK to clean out your intestines, but it isn't really considered a food group," he said seriously as he exited through the cat door. "You have to be careful what you eat out here, so follow me," he continued as he led me off the deck with his tail pointed in the air, exposing me to his least attractive feature.

Although I tagged along after him, I was only pretending to listen. He was telling me more than I ever wanted to know about Northern Virginia's fauna, and I was anxious to go off on my own. I felt invincible and couldn't imagine any inanimate object being a threat to me, so I just nodded my head and turned on the "uh-huh" machine to make Bobby think I was listening while I daydreamed about mice, moles, and other lesser forms of life.

Bobby's guided tour of the yard seemed to take forever, but it only lasted an hour. All that talk about what I could and couldn't eat made me hungry, but I was so relieved to be out, I didn't want to go inside for lunch. So I resigned myself to remaining hungry. Talk about missing the point!

We lived in a nice, civilized neighborhood where garbage was well contained, so dumpster diving for "fast food" wasn't an option. Finally, I thought of the obvious; I'd search

17

outdoors for natural foods like Bobby and Ewle Gibbons did. It occurred to me that I should have been listening more carefully to Bobby's lecture on the subject, but I was sure my instincts would guide me to a suitable *al fresco* snack. Sniffing the ground, I discovered a brown object that smelled pretty good — although a little earthy. I took a bite. "Not bad." So I made a pig of myself on mushroom appetizers.

It wasn't an hour later that I started feeling incredibly sick to my stomach. "Oh, oh," I thought. "Maybe I should have listened to Bobby. This is what I get for not paying attention."

I made it into the house just in time to throw up all over the white living room carpet. Then another wave of nausea hit, forcing me to regurgitate again, only this time on the sofa. Throwing up on carpeting or upholstery was an instinctual thing — like always landing on my feet when I fell. No one actually taught me to do it; whenever I felt myself getting sick, I was somehow mystically drawn to interior furnishings.

As it turned out, the poison mushrooms I'd consumed kept me sick and housebound for the rest of the day. While recuperating curled up on the hot air vent, I overheard Bobby talking to Nathan about me in the most derogatory terms. He despaired of kittens, he said, because we were so stubborn, selfish and stupid, not necessarily in that order. Nathan was much more tolerant. He gently reminded Bobby that we were all alike — old-timers like himself and newcomers like me. Kittens were just small cats with less experience. Nathan assured Bobby that I'd learn — in time.

I knew I must really be bad because only The Won spent any time with me while I was sick. Bobby was angry because I'd ignored his nature lecture, and Billy and Angus went about their business as if I were invisible. My feelings were hurt and I told Nathan so.

"What do you expect, Fred?" Nathan replied. "When you're well, you don't pay any attention to them. You always have something better to do. And on the few occasions when you play with Billy and Angus, you bully them into doing what you want to do. You never ask them what they want."

Nathan's words didn't improve my mood. I wanted sympathy, not the truth. I walked down the hall and saw that the bathroom door was closed, so I started scratching at it furiously. I took two layers of paint off the jam before I stopped. I really didn't care about getting into the bathroom or what lay beyond the door. I scratched at the door because it was there and it was closed. "I scratch, therefore I am," I boasted, even though I knew my claw marks would infuriate The Won.

"What's wrong with me anyway?" I finally asked myself, feeling ashamed. I wanted the others to like me and, more importantly, I wanted to like myself. Yet during the past week, I'd violated curfew rather than compromise my "freedom"; I'd ignored Bobby's help and suffered the physical consequences; and I'd damaged my own house (in addition to my reputation), upsetting The Won, my best friend in the whole world. My behavior was no longer acceptable to me. As much as I hated the thought of improving my character, it was time to admit that I needed to change — and that I needed help being shown how.

19

Chapter Three
The Family Circle

It was 4 p.m. and time for "school" with Nathan and Bobby. "Hi, I'm Humpty Dumpty and I'm here to be put back together again," I said joining them in the den. Unfortunately they didn't see the humor in my analogy. Our sessions still included prayer and meditation, which served to center me, but the emphasis was now on my new "life lessons." My mentors considered me so socially-challenged, they started my education by teaching me some pretty elementary manners.

I learned that it was not polite to sit on the dining room table when The Won had guests, for example, much less be observed bathing on it. I should avoid coughing up furballs immediately before, during and after dinner. I was not to sleep in the same bed as The Won's overnight guests unless I was specifically invited. I shouldn't wash my privates before bestowing cat kisses on The Won or any other human. A soft meow followed by intense concentration on an object was the proper way to request it. Conversely, clawing The Won's leg for attention was to be avoided at all costs, lest I receive the kind of attention I didn't want — followed by an immediate assist outside. The cardinal rule, of course, was "always come when you're called" — "within reason" was left unsaid.

Regarding my peers, I was advised never to join any of them while they were using the communal kitty litter; always completely cover anything I left in the litter (including toys); never bite anyone hard enough to puncture their skin or leave telltale tooth impressions; and never "nose" anyone out of their

20

dish while they were still eating, although I was free to graze after they walked away. (Bobby actually blushed when we got to this last rule which he was guilty of violating on a regular basis, although he did it in a very clever way. When all our dishes of food were put down, Bobby quickly made the rounds and took a few bites out of each before any of us had a chance to sit down to dinner. This did not constitute a technical violation and explained why Bobby was so portly.)

I kept watching the clock, waiting for our hour together to pass like a stubborn kidney stone. I was delighted when fate intervened in the form of a ringing telephone. The Won never interrupted us by coming into the den to answer the phone, because it normally never rang — until evening when the telemarketers knew it was the dinner hour.

"Hi boys!" The Won greeted us smiling, as he walked by to get to the phone. Remaining quiet so we could eavesdrop, we listened to a very one-sided conversation. "When? How? What can I do?" The Won questioned the caller. It didn't take a genius to see how overwrought he was becoming.

When The Won got off the phone, he looked sadder than I'd ever seen him. "One of our friends died, boys," he confided, as he told us how his oldest friend, Bob, had succumbed to a heart attack. He thought we'd be interested because Bob was one of several long-term house guests he'd entertained last year. (Well, *entertained* was perhaps the wrong word — so was *house guest* for that matter. These were male friends of The Won who casually stopped by for a visit in between life engagements. They set up residence in the back bedroom and stayed for months at a time, leaving only their socks and some loose change as evidence of their trespass.)

21

I never knew Bob, but the others said they liked him. He truly disliked cats, which is what attracted us to him. My siblings sat on him, rubbed up against him, and even trained him to fill their dishes, although they suspected Bob fed them in order to get rid of them rather than to win their affection. But that was neither here nor there. Now Bob was gone; The Won was sad; and our job was to be extra affectionate for awhile.

The very next day, we were in the middle of another lesson in the den when the phone rang again. We looked at each other, all thinking the same thing. The Won took the call, acknowledging the caller. This couldn't be happening a second time, I thought, but it was. Stephen, another of The Won's long-term guests last year, was also dead. In Stephen's case, his indifference to us was reciprocated, but we all felt badly anyway. We knew how painful this was for The Won, who was the same age as both Stephen and Bob (in human years). No wonder The Won was so upset! Talk about being made aware of your mortality!

We rallied around The Won, who appeared calm, but his eyes were strangely glazed. He didn't respond when Nathan rubbed up against him, so I decided to try comforting The Won. I don't know what made me think I could reach through The Won's pain when Nathan, his true soulmate, couldn't — inflated ego, I guess.

The Won got up, went into his bedroom, and closed the door. We didn't see him again until nightfall when he was attired in his "comfort" sweater. When The Won was physically sick, he stayed in his pajamas and avoided standard hygiene practices; when he was emotionally sick with the "laying down disease," he wore his comfort sweater and ate comfort food like mashed potatoes, pudding, and chicken soup. At the moment, both life and chewing were proving too difficult for The Won it seemed.

The next morning everyone except Nathan gathered in the kitchen in front of our cafeteria line of dishes, but they were all empty — and there was no evidence of The Won in sight. We formed a chorus and called him in unison, but there was still no response. The Won was sometimes prone to selective hearing, but usually not when it came to feeding us. We looked at each other in disbelief. It was true the dry food dispenser was full, as it always was, so we were never in danger of starving, but The Won *never* forgot to give us ample helpings of our shrimp and fish cassoulet. This was serious!

Pretty soon Nathan descended the stairs very slowly, his limp appearing more pronounced than usual. Instead of being respectful of Nathan's presence in bed, The Won had pulled the covers so taut, so quickly, that Nathan, who was lying on top of them, was launched into space like a rocket. It was only luck that he "touched down" on the bed instead of the hardwood floor, but he still suffered minor bruising as well as major emotional trauma. I was appalled at The Won's callousness!

The Won's neglect intensified over the next few days. He regularly forgot to empty our litter, fill our dishes, or occasionally provide us with catnip. He didn't even bother calling us in at 10 p.m., forcing us to police ourselves and each other. I was sympathetic at first, but now I was annoyed. So what if The Won's friends had "lived, loved, laughed and left?" Life was fatal, and that was a fact! We all had to go sometime. The Won had better get used to the idea. Sympathy obviously wasn't one of my strong suits.

23

Nathan took the opposite tact. He told us we'd have to try harder than ever before to ingratiate ourselves. We'd kill The Won with kindness to re-ignite his interest in us. Nathan suggested that Angus bow with his chin to the floor, then scoot along after The Won in what became known as "assuming the position." He asked Billy to stand on his hind legs and beg when The Won came into the kitchen in order to amuse The Won (while reminding him to feed us — a nicer approach than constantly whining at him). Nathan suggested that Bobby learn to roll over, a demonstration of humility which Bobby was willing but unable to do. Because of his girth, Bobby got stuck in mid-roll and, instead of looking cute, he looked rather pathetic. I volunteered to do "roll-overs" instead, but despite our efforts to be irresistible, The Won didn't respond and remained as aloof as before.

Nathan was our acknowledged conduit to the "hairless" world, so we respected his opinion and followed his suggestions, whether they produced results or not. Even when I doubted Nathan's ability to convert The Won back into a life form, I still did what he said because "in the land of the blind, the one-eyed man is king." My job of rolling over every time The Won came into view was getting monotonous and depressing, so I kept my spirits up by whistling the theme song from "The Bridge Over The River Kwai." This worked initially, until the atmosphere in the Clarke household became so oppressive for so long that, when I looked in the mirror, I saw Alec Guinness staring back at me.

"What to do? What to do? What to do?" I mused. Having lost faith in Nathan's solution, I decided to implement a plan of my own — without anyone else's help. It was Nathan who always said, "Don't tell me how you feel or what you think; tell me what you're doing about it." Not only was I going to take action, I was going to take action on someone else's behalf. Talk about growth!

Months ago Nathan had posed a riddle to me. "How many sides has a circle?" he asked. I admitted I didn't know (and prided myself on stopping short of telling him that I also didn't care). Nathan answered his own question: "Two — the inside and the outside," adding that I'd be much happier if I stayed on the inside of our family circle. I'd already made the emotional commitment to doing just that, but first I had to try my best to repair the tear in its circumference.

A mature, thoughtful Nathan.

25

Chapter Four
The Goose

Despite intellectually knowing better, I still suffered hurt feelings over The Won's indifference. When I tried to get his attention, he just shooed me away. "So screw him," I thought, ducking my head through the cat door and marching outside where Nathan was sunning himself.

Nathan's chin was resting on his front paws and, although he didn't open his eyes immediately, he sensed I was there. "What's happening, Fred?"

"Nothing," I said dejectedly.

"I hope you're not still brooding over The Won. You need to understand that his attitude has nothing to do with you," Nathan said in a matter-of-fact tone.

"It makes me angry that he doesn't care about us anymore. What did we do, anyway? It's not fair," I pouted.

"Fred, you aren't listening. This is about him, not about us. He's angry and sad that his best friends are dying and he's afraid of his own mortality. He's not himself. He's depressed."

"What's depressed?" I asked, really wanting to know.

"Well, depression is like anger without enthusiasm." Nathan explained. "It takes the wind out of your sails; it darkens your vision; it leaves a hole in your soul."

"Will he ever get better?" I asked hopefully.

"I think so, Fred, but we are all powerless over his depression — and if you need 'powerless' defined, it's 'lacking the ability to surmount or overcome something.' So for right now, just be as understanding and as helpful as you can. We need to act like geese."

"Huh?" I said intelligently. What did a bunch of birds with overactive thyroids have to do with us? I thought.

"Did you ever watch the way geese fly in a 'V' formation? They do that because as each bird flaps its wings it creates an uplift for the bird that's immediately behind it," Nathan said. "Geese know that if they stay together they make flight easier for each other. In a way, the same can be said for families. We also have to stick together to make life easier," Nathan soothed.

"When the head goose gets tired, it rotates to the back of the formation and another goose comes up to fly 'point.' The geese honk from behind to encourage those up front to keep up their speed — the same way we encourage each other when one of us is experiencing difficulty. Finally, when a goose gets sick or is wounded by gunshot and falls out of formation, two other geese fall out with the incapacitated goose and follow it down until it's able to fly again or until it dies. Only then do they leave it to resume their journey with another formation or to catch up with the original one."

"Think of our family as a gaggle of geese, Fred," Nathan continued. "The Won is wounded, so I'll be taking the lead for awhile. And Angus and Billy are staying with The

27

Won until he feels better, which I'm sure he eventually will —
it's just a matter of time."

Talking to Nathan always helped me to think more
clearly. If The Won's problem was losing friends, I logically
concluded that all he needed was some new friends to replace
the ones he'd lost. So I decided to go out and find The Won a
new friend or two. That was it! I was sure I'd stumbled on the
cure for what ailed The Won! He needed new friends!

As I completed that thought, I heard honking from
above as a gaggle of geese flew by in "V" formation, just like
Nathan had described. Talk about divine inspiration! I was
receiving a message directly from my Higher Meower! So I
raced from the deck and flew across the lawn, en route to
bringing home The Won's first new friend — a goose.

I knew where the gaggle hung out — by the pond on the
golf course — because I'd seen them there many times, leaving
cigar-sized droppings on the impeccably-groomed greens and
fairways, much to the chagrin of cleat-footed golfers. I thought
it would be easy to "cut one out from the herd," but as soon as I
came near a goose, it and its closest friends honked, flapped
their wings in unison, rose a foot or two off the ground, and
flew the few feet to the pond before effortlessly skidding to a
stop in the water.

I made two more efforts to separate the least intelligent-
looking bird from the gaggle, but the result was always the
same. More and more geese fled to the pond where I couldn't
follow. Doing the same thing over and over and expecting a
different result was insane, so I decided to set my sights a little
lower. Perhaps a smaller bird, less noble and more susceptible

28

to manipulation, was the answer (and there were plenty of those right around our house).

It was rumored that some humans actually kept birds as pets; though, for the life of me, I couldn't understand why. I didn't think of myself as prejudiced or superior, but — hello— the term "bird-brained" said it all. Chattering a baby sparrow down from its perch, I proved my point before harmlessly pouncing on it and tenderly carrying it home in my mouth.

I was relieved when I finally arrived at my cat door, shoved my head through it, and spit out the struggling mass of feathers at The Won's feet. I don't know who was more surprised by my thoughtfulness — The Won or the bird — because they were both as wide-eyed as baby deer caught in the headlights of an oncoming car. When The Won picked up the bird, I was sure my instinct to bring him his first new friend was right on target, but the bird was so nervous, it pooped all over his hand. As soon as The Won verified that the bird was uninjured, he set it free. Although I was a tad disappointed, in some respects, I was relieved The Won's taste in "friends" was more discriminating than I at first believed.

As I saw it, my mistake hadn't been bringing The Won a new friend. My mistake had been bringing him the *wrong* new friend. So I set out once again, looking for an animal that would capture The Won's imagination and re-ignite his interest in all of us. I considered going after a mole. They aren't very cute and they're virtually blind, I conceded, but their redeeming feature is that they don't go around feeling sorry for themselves. Despite their handicap, they are very industrious, digging hundreds of holes in the ground connected by a complex series of tunnels. I knew how much The Won admired ordinary workers — he was always talking about being a worker among workers — even though he didn't particularly like moles.

At one point, The Won had actually tried to rid the yard of moles by putting toy plastic windmills in the ground next to their holes. The windmills were supposed to make the ground vibrate, thereby driving the moles from their tunnels, but these colorful devices attracted even more moles to the yard — fun-loving moles who enjoyed residing in a Disney-like environment. Eventually The Won was forced to adopt a "live and let live" policy concerning the moles, whom he begrudgingly admired for their tenacity and desire for upward mobility.

It wasn't easy catching a mole. I had to exercise an inordinate amount of patience waiting for one to emerge from its hole, but my patience finally paid off. The end result of my efforts, however, was the same as with the bird. Once The Won made sure the mole wasn't injured, he released it.

Because I was sure my plan to find The Won new friends was a direct result of divine inspiration, it never occurred to me to ask Bobby or Nathan what they thought about my project. I was sure my motives were pure, even though I wanted to keep all the credit for myself. I didn't realize that I was guilty of self-aggrandizement. I was sincere about wanting The Won to be happy again, but mistaken in the belief that I was the only one who could make that happen.

I continued to rely solely on my own counsel as I sought my next candidate, Angus' friend, the squirrel. Angus and the squirrel had studiously been ignoring each other for months while they inched closer and closer on the deck, testing each other's intentions. One day the squirrel was hanging upside down drinking water from a flower pot when Angus got *thisclose* to him. When the squirrel came up for air, the two animals inadvertently bumped into one another, scaring themselves silly. However, since the incident, they seemed much less skittish. I was sure the squirrel would like living with us, but I hadn't considered what it would be like living with him. No sooner had he moved in than he ate through the telephone wires and TV cable, leaving us electronically impaired. He was invited to leave shortly thereafter.

Next, I herded home an opossum who sorely lacked social skills, spitting and swearing at both myself and The Won as it demonstrated its contempt for captivity and us. My last effort was a baby racoon whose mother became violent when I attempted to separate her from her offspring. Thank goodness Nathan interceded on my behalf, chasing away the mother racoon before she had a chance to *really* hurt me.

Every night for a week thereafter, Nathan was curiously attendant to me, following me wherever I went and checking up on me. I thought his behavior strange until Bobby explained that many racoons in the area carried rabies, which made animals crazy. If the mother coon who'd taken a nip out of me was rabid, I'd come down with the disease as well. Nathan confided to Bobby that watching me to see if I was crazy wasn't as cut and dried as it might seem. Often he couldn't tell one way or the other, but at least I wasn't foaming at the mouth, a good sign.

I finally concluded that it just wasn't in the cards for me to find a new friend for The Won. Instead of feeling like a failure, however, I patted myself on the back for my maturity.

I'd learned that when things worked out the way I planned, it was God's will, and that when things didn't work out the way I planned, it was also God's will.

Nathan boasted that his efforts to help others were at least 50% successful. When I asked him how he knew that, I expected him to give me a scientific explanation based on the total number of creatures he tried to help versus the number of successes he enjoyed, but he simply replied: "Anytime I attempt to help another, I am at least 50% successful because I am always helped."

So I, too, had been 50% successful. And although I may not have rekindled The Won's attentiveness or affection for us, at least he wasn't sitting in that big chair looking forlorn and feeling sorry for himself anymore. My efforts kept him on his toes, capturing the creatures I brought home, and he remained in a state of full alert for some time to come, just in case I wasn't through yet.

The Won's depression was one more unresolved problem with which I learned to be at peace and, in the meantime, I gained a bit of self-esteem by doing "esteem-able" things to try to help him. I realized I wasn't the celebrity of my dreams, but neither was I the nobody of my nightmares. I'd tried to do something for someone else, even though I was a bit misguided in my total self-reliance, old behavior for which I apologized to Nathan and Bobby.

"Fred," Nathan said, "If you're still doing it, it's not *old* behavior."

Chapter Five
School Daze

It was a particularly warm March day and I'd spent most of the morning on the deck basking in the sun with Billy and Angus. Angus' constant chatter usually annoyed me but, since he could no longer carry on endless conversations with The Won, I tried to be more tolerant. I was grateful to be a member of this large, loving family, and when I was grateful I was always serene, i.e. at peace with myself and in harmony with others. Nathan said peace of mind was God's nod of approval.

When I was disenfranchised and hungry, angry, lonely and tired, I was sure the God of my misunderstanding had abandoned me out of anger and disappointment. I was reminded of the Biblical joke Bobby told about Job, upon whom befell one tragedy after another. Finally, desperate to understand why all these bad things were happening to him, such a good and faithful servant, Job beseeched God, "Why me, why me?" In answer to his question, God's booming voice descended from the heavens: "Because there's just something about you that pisses me off!" Today I could appreciate the humor of that joke but, before I started my prayer and meditation sessions with Nathan and Bobby, the only God I knew was Job's punishing God.

I was thankful my lessons with Nathan and Bobby covered practical as well as spiritual matters because I needed both. In addition to learning about the seven deadly sins, I was also taught about manners and appropriate behavior. I have to admit that being considerate of others was never a priority of mine. To be truthful, I had a "me first — if-you-snooze-you-lose" attitude when it came to getting what I wanted.

Bobby taught me that the seven deadly sins were instincts used for more than their intended purpose, and that good character traits usually turned into bad character defects when taken to the extreme. He said a trait turned into a defect when it was harmful or resulted in irresponsibility.

Good Trait	Bad Defect
Responsibility	**Control**
You make the effort to take care of yourself	You think you're responsible for the outcome of that effort
Self-Esteem	**Self-Absorption**
You think a lot *of* yourself	You think *only* of yourself
Humility	**Humiliation**
You *recognize* your deficiencies	You *demonstrate* your deficiencies
Rest	**Sloth**
A respite from work	A total avoidance of work
Love	**Lust**
Intimacy often resulting in sex	Sex seldom resulting in intimacy
Helpfulness	**Martyrdom**
Selfless assistance resulting in satisfaction	Selfish assistance resulting in resentment
Anger	**Rage**
Ill feeling expressed as displeasure	Ill feeling defying reasonable expression
Pleasure/Happiness/Joy	**Ecstasy**
Physical/emotional/spiritual by-products of right living	Unearned joy, often a mental by-product of drugs or delusion.

Sadness	**Depression**
Situational feeling of loss or dejection	Often inexplicable, debilitating feeling of loss or dejection
Empathy/Sympathy	**Pathos**
Understanding/feeling how someone else feels	Suffering someone else's tragedies
Willing	**Wanting**
Taking action to achieve a result	Hoping for a result without taking action
Rigorous Honesty	**Brutal Honesty**
Self-examination for a clear conscience	Microscopic examination with no conscience
Regret/Remorse	**Guilt/Shame**
Sorrow you were bad	Belief that you are bad
Excitement	**Agitation**
Emotion stirred by anticipation	Emotion stirred by irritation
Ambition	**Greed**
Desire to have something	Need to have everything
Hunger	**Gluttony**
The stimulous to eat something	The act of eating everything
Admiration	**Envy**
Wanting what someone else possesses	Wanting someone else's possessions
Pride	**False Pride**
Self-respect	Self-delusion
Perseverance	**Obstinacy**
Strong Will	Strong Won't
Grace	**Justice**
Getting something I don't deserve	Getting something I do deserve

I was really beginning to like these lessons, but I also couldn't help wonder why I was the only recipient of them. Billy and Angus never participated, and no one even hinted that they should. Nathan suggested that I was just lucky. He said I should accept the fact that I'd been *chosen*. When I asked him, "chosen for what?" He replied "retooling." He said if I looked at myself like a factory, I'd been producing an inferior product (self-centeredness) and was being retooled for a better product (virtuous behavior).

Noticing my lack of enthusiasm for that particular analogy, Bobby jumped in with one of his own. He said that virtuous behavior was simply being the best Fred I could be and helping others — like a Samurai warrior. While I relished the image of myself as a slant-eyed, silken-sashed, sword-carrying Samurai, I didn't understand what that had to do with helping others until Bobby explained that the English translation of "samurai" was "to serve." Their analogies were driving me nuts!

Chapter Six
Ginger and Fred

I loved the smell of spring in the air and could hardly wait for morning. As soon as the sun kissed the sky and dawn appeared through the cracks in the bedroom blackout shutters, I'd burst forth from the cat door in the dining room out on to the deck to watch my neighborhood awaken. I took particular pleasure trying to lure the twittering birds, alarm clocks to the world, from their perches in the trees.

Bobby was the only other member of the house who was up and awake, his motivation to feed his rumbling stomach. Like clockwork, he awoke every morning at 6 a.m., ready for breakfast. He'd learned that by executing a quick series of jumping jacks on The Won's chest, he could coerce The Won out of bed to feed us. The Won resented this intrusion at first, but soon became adept at stumbling to the kitchen, filling our dishes, finding his way back up the stairs and returning to bed without ever opening his eyes.

Bobby had a habit of grazing in everyone's dish except mine, which I protected by keeping my face in it until it was empty. Nathan, Billy and Angus stayed in bed with The Won until he finished his second phase of sleeping, which gave Bobby the opportunity to inhale most of their food. I greedily dispensed with mine so I could get on with my day because, unlike Bobby who lived to eat, I simply ate to live.

I didn't understand how the others could be so cavalier about dawn, much less about spring. I was truly a morning creature and welcomed the warming temperatures. Of course the others had experienced many more springs than I — this was actually the first that I remembered. Last year I wasn't old enough to notice the nuances of seasons, but today I loved to sniff around, investigating the different types of buds trying to break ground. I felt a sense of anticipation that was new to me, like I was poised at the edge of a precipice beyond which lay something wonderful, even though I didn't have a clue as to what it might be.

I'd done a lot of growing in the last year, if not growing up. (Bobby insisted that I'd only be young once, but I would probably stay immature forever.) I attributed his comment to jealousy since my physical growth had been proportional instead of primarily outward like Bobby's. I was longer and leaner, having passed puberty and emerged into adolescence. All of my senses were more alert; I was a lean, mean, feline machine — a divining rod in search of something divine. Restless but happy, I was anticipative, anxious for life's next adventure.

I loved to feel the grass brush by me as I stalked my imagination en route to the front yard where I watched the activity in our *cul-de-sac* below. Well hidden in the tall grass, I was thankful The Won hadn't yet mowed it this season. Feeling like James Bond, I peered across the street to where a moving van had been parked the previous day. Moving vans were pretty common in our neighborhood and, for that matter, all over greater Washington, D.C. becaue of its large transient community of military, foreign service and political personnel.

Both Nathan and Bobby had warned me to stay away from moving vans, which had a reputation for capturing curious cats and inadvertently transporting them cross-country. Although I'd heard The Won talk about other parts of the country, I didn't particularly want to be relocated to any of them, especially alone and by accident. So I stayed perched on my hill until the new neighbors were safely moved into their house, after which I became a one-creature welcome wagon paying them the first of many courtesy calls.

Lightly bounding down our stucco wall (I never took the stairs), I was pleased to see that the neighbors hadn't hung their curtains yet. Sitting on the outside ledge of the picture window, I was able to look into the house and get a clear view of the living room, dining room and kitchen. I hadn't heard the sounds of telltale barking, so I was fairly certain the family didn't have a dog. ("Thank God," I thought. There were already three dogs in the *cul-de-sac* and that was three too many as far as I was concerned.)

Pressing my nose to the window, my eyes swept the floorboards like a dustmop, hoping to spot a resident animal. It was difficult to see around the cardboard boxes that cluttered the floor. I thought I spotted something under the chair across the room and squinted so I could see better. I was concentrating so hard, I almost had a heart attack when, with a loud thud, a cat landed on its feet right in front of me, separated only by the window pane.

I was so startled, I fell off the edge of the planter, right into the privet bush below. Embarrassed, I shook myself off before leaping back on the ledge, now nose-to-nose with the most attractive redhead I'd ever seen. It was my first "she" and, boy, was she a beauty! I could smell "the scent of a woman" right through the thick window pane.

"Ooo-wah," I was as captivated by her as she seemed enamored of me. (Well, perhaps "enamored" was too strong a word, but at least she didn't hate me because her back wasn't humped, her fur wasn't standing on end, and she wasn't spitting or hissing. Although if she'd been doing all three, I probably wouldn't have let that deter my ardor. Who said liking me had to be a criteria for a relationship?) Her greeting was low and guttural, almost sexy, and I definitely perceived a "come hither" look in her eye.

We exchanged only a few words, but enough for me to find out her name was Ginger. My head swam. "Ginger and Fred...Fred and Ginger," it had a familiar ring to it. She said she wouldn't be allowed out for at least a week, the usual acclimation period humans provided for their pets to adjust to a new neighborhood, but we could "dance" together in the meantime, separated only by the window pane. It was clear she was a romantic, picturing this tuxedo cat twirling her in circles, her long red fur shimmering in the breeze. I was too, but I balked at only being able to fantasize about her for a week; I wanted to see her eye-to-eye and smell her nose-to-nose — right now! Patience wasn't a strong suit of mine.

I was sorely tempted to break into her house and I told her so, but she discouraged me. She said we could meet every day at this same spot and start to get to know each other. She called this "dating." It would serve to heighten the anticipation of getting together for the first time, she said, as she assured me she was worth waiting for. I couldn't stand it. I howled!

I never felt my feet touch the ground as I floated back up the retaining wall and into the house to look for Nathan. From what the others told me, Nathan had a girlfriend — Kitty

40

— who lived in the house diagonally across the street (kitty-cornered, so to speak). There was no point asking Bobby, Billy or Angus about females. Bobby was the only one who had any experience with the opposite sex, and it was all bad!

I raced through the cat door, across the dining and living rooms, up the stairs, and found Nathan in the den, lying on the floor in a patch of sunlight below the photograph of him and BR. I couldn't help notice how young and handsome Nathan had been in that photograph, taken so many years ago. He was lean and buff, his facial features hard and chiseled. I wondered if I should be asking advice on modern relationships from someone his age. How could his story of "what it used to be like, what happened, and what it was like now" possibly still be pertinent?

His views on courtship were probably very old-fashioned, but I had nowhere else to go for advice. Once I told Nathan about Ginger and asked him what to do next, I closed my mouth, opened my mind, and listened to what he had to say. This approach had worked successfully in the past on other matters, so why not now, on a matter of the heart?

Nathan slowly got up on all fours, looked at me with interest, turned in a tight circle, then sat down again in the very same spot from which he arose. I could tell this was going to be a lengthy "lesson," since it was preceded by his necessity to rearrange himself. I made myself comfortable next to him and tried to keep my eyes open. (Whenever I listened with my eyes closed, I had a habit of falling asleep.)

Nathan cleared his throat and began. "Hmmm, where to start?" he said, as much to himself as to me.

41

"Oh, oh," I thought. "That's as bad as someone saying 'To make a long story short,' which it then never was." When Nathan asked how much I knew about the birds and the bees, I volunteered that I once spent hours watching them with Billy and had concluded that their entertainment value was vastly over-rated.

I saw the hint of a smile on Nathan's face as he told me that's not what he meant. So starting from the beginning, Nathan explained adolescence, the changes it had already wrought on my body, and more than I ever wanted to know about the clinical side of sex and procreation — which surely would have dashed my enthusiasm were it not for my already raging hormones and lustful thoughts of Ginger.

Differentiating between love and lust wasn't easy, Nathan said, because both climaxed in the same physical act; the difference was the time and attention devoted to the act. Love, he explained, was usually multi-dimensional and long-lasting, often resulting in a future together, while lust was characterized by instant gratification and usually limited to a one-night stand (or series of them).

The first stage of a relationship was like a speeding car, out of control. Raging hormones produced a sense of euphoria, excitement and anticipation. No matter what the object of your affections did or said, it was fascinating. There weren't enough hours in the day to spend with him or her. Any idiosyncracies or oddities that surfaced were dismissed out of hand or deemed charming. This phase lasted up to four months, Nathan said.

Next was the discovery phase when reality began to dawn. Those "charming" idiosyncracies were beginning to annoy you. You wondered what other flaws were left to uncover. Your euphoria was becoming tainted by other emotions as you wrestled with the question of commitment. You'd slammed on the brakes of that speeding car, and all the junk from the back seat came tumbling forward to hit you on the head …selfishness, jealousy, fear, etc. Your emotions surged as you wrestled with the decision to either advance the relationship further or get out while there was still time — before you got hurt. You revisited this issue whenever your partner didn't meet your expectations until "getting out" was no longer an option. You discovered you were already committed, even though that hadn't been your intention — but it beat the alternative of being alone again.

The process sounded utterly exhausting, I thought!

Nathan cleared his throat again. "If you decide to always give your partner the benefit of the doubt, accept both the good and the bad, enjoy her differences as well as the things you share in common, be willing to change your mind, and be more interested in being happy than right, you're on your way to a truly special, intimate and rewarding relationship, one that's built on a firm foundation of lasting love. Nathan smiled, looking like Robert Young, as he described this final stage as "a special bond with another creature to whom you are so closely allied that your immediate instinct is always to seek them out when you have good news, bad news, or any news at all, because they truly are your partner in life."

"Whew," I was sorry I asked. This was serious business — too serious; it didn't sound like any fun at all. "I'm only a little more than a year old. Can't I just have sex with her?" I hadn't intended to blurt out this last thought, which resulted

43

from panic at the prospect of a commitment that lasted more than a few minutes.

Nathan looked resigned rather than surprised. "Unfortunately, we don't have a very good reputation for lasting relationships within our species," he conceded. "Just make sure you're honest with her and you both agree that's all you want."

In an uncharacteristic moment of self-honesty, I knew I was more suited to the role of frequent father than *Father Knows Best*. "OK," I said getting up quickly before Nathan had a chance to elaborate. I hoped Ginger wasn't getting similar advice about "relationships," and raced out of the room as though my tail were on fire! Nathan, of course, knew what I didn't — that my interest in such matters would soon be out of my control and decidedly in the hands of The Won.

But for now, I faithfully reported to the window ledge outside Ginger's living room every day for a week like it was a full-time job. She always appeared on the other side of the window pane, looking well-groomed and as eager as I was to meet nose-to-nose. When we finally did, it was almost anti-climactic — until we had sex, that is.

We spent the next few weeks locked together like Rubics Cube, an experience which I felt Nathan vastly under-rated in his description of it. Sex was more mind-blowing than I could ever have imagined, at least the "fitzrowring," screeching, grass-shredding, earth-clawing variety I enjoyed with Ginger. It was so good, in fact, the more I had, the more I wanted. So I naturally went looking for additional sources to "double my pleasure and double my fun." And, much to my amazement, I found another partner as ready and willing as Ginger. When I mentioned this to Nathan, he referred to me as a "moral-free zone."

I became like a heat-seeking missile as far as females were concerned. I was delirious, invincible, and amazed at how popular I was. I'd always felt like such a runt, but with each new conquest, I became taller, bigger, smarter. Pretty soon I was so puffed up, I could hardly fit through my cat door, but that was actually OK because I never came home anyway.

After another chat with Nathan concerning my morals, I really started feeling guilty about "catting" around — primarily with Ginger and Flossy, who conveniently lived on opposite sides of the neighborhood. Neither knew about the other and, up to now, I justified my behavior as monogamous because I was only seeing them one at a time.

Nathan tried telling me a human parable to illustrate the nature of my wrongs with regard to my sex conduct — it had something to do with a Mr. Brown and a Mrs. Jones, but I wasn't listening. I didn't need to. Whenever I spent a lot of time rationalizing my behavior, it was usually because it was misbehavior. I knew I was totally selfish, self-absorbed and self-centered, but it seemed a small price to pay for popularity. Besides, Nathan's views were old-fashioned, I was convinced.

Because Nathan wouldn't endorse my seeing Ginger, Flossy, and a variety of others simultaneously, I decided to get a second opinion from someone younger, more with it, and with more recent experience — Bobby. I often sought a second opinion when I didn't like the first. Unfortunately, they almost never differed and this was no exception.

45

Bobby's history included only one relationship — with a cute Calico — but it had turned out badly. He admitted that the anticipation of their union was much more exciting than the actual event. He was almost glad when The Won had him "fixed," so he'd never have to ride that emotional roller coaster again. (I didn't understand the word "fixed," but I didn't want to interrupt the flow of Bobby's story to ask.)

Bobby said the relationship started out being very sweet. He described their early courtship when he'd accepted everything about her, including her past. When he first saw her he thought she was a lot younger than she turned out to be. Her stretch marks were a clue that she'd been around and had produced a litter or two in her youth. When she described her home life, he felt sorry for her. She had an owner, but few of the perks of being a pet. Her owner fairly ignored her, creating within her a desperation for love and any sign of affection.

Bobby said he wasn't prejudiced about May-December relationships, so their age difference wasn't a factor in the break-up. He said it wasn't long before some of her habits, which he originally found "cute" and endearing, became annoying. He got irritated by the way she chewed her food, using the side of her mouth because of a broken fang. He was also embarrassed by the way she blatantly bathed her "privates" in public.

He really cared for her, however, and offered numerous suggestions on how she could improve herself, but instead of being grateful, she cheated on him with the black and white tom who lived on the corner of 35th and Vermont. Bobby was devastated when he found out, and went into an emotional tailspin to which he referred as being "Candy-coated," but by

46

the time he saw her a few weeks later, he was over her. It seems she'd gotten fat. She also bragged about moving — to the beach — although he suspected she was lying.

"Oh my God," I thought. "My mother was a calico named Candy! Oh my God," I thought again. "My mother's owner didn't treat her very well, and she was forced to move out when she became pregnant with me and my sisters. Oh my God," my brain exploded with the realization that Bobby was talking about my mother!

I stared at Bobby, my mouth open in disbelief. I remembered when Nathan was explaining the facts of life to me and said that females could be impregnated by more than one male at the same time — the reason their litters sometimes resembled variety packs. If Bobby was sleeping with my mother the same time she was sleeping with the black and white tom who lived on the corner of 35th and Vermont, and she was "fat" the next time he saw her, she was obviously pregnant — by both of them. I asked Bobby when that happened, then counted how old I was on my paws. "Oh my God," I realized, "Bobby is one of my fathers!"

"What's the matter Fred?" Bobby said, noticing the look of amazement in my eyes and the fact that the color had literally drained from my face, leaving me albino.

For the first time in my life, I was speechless and my heart was beating a mile a minute. My Momcat told me my daddy was a black and white tom who was a traveling man, but she never mentioned she was seeing someone else at the same time — although I should have known. Now it all made sense, because while one of my sisters was black and white, exactly like me, the other two were dark blonde and looked exactly like Bobby.

"Daddy!" I yelled as I jumped on Bobby.

Later that evening I thought how fitting it was that it had been Bobby who'd saved my life and brought me home. As I curled up between him and my Uncle Billy, I said my prayers to my Higher Meower. I now realized how He'd always been working in my life. Nathan told me there would come a time when I would truly trust my Higher Meower and understand just how much He loved me, and this was it. How could I possibly doubt that love or the fact that He carried me through the tough times when I remembered how I'd gotten here? Nathan said there were no coincidences. Coincidences were God working anonymously.

My eyes misted as I remembered how Bobby first spotted me at the top of the hill stealing the food meant for the racoons and how he brought me kibbles every day to supplement my diet, carrying them stuffed in his cheeks, just like a squirrel with its nuts.

It was a miracle Bobby decided to take me home by the scruff of my neck when I was so weak I couldn't even walk. Tomcats weren't known for their compassion toward other tomcats — although I was hardly a threat in my condition. I knew Bobby was as aware of the miraculous nature of our reunion as I was, because he had tears in his eyes when he looked at me.

When I'd questioned Nathan why my Higher Meower had permitted me to be mistreated when I was a kitten, Nathan explained that my Higher Meower had nothing to do with that mistreatment. Tiger had been evil and that's all there was to it! Beyond understanding that, I needn't bother trying to understand my Higher Meower or God, because a God small enough for me to understand wasn't big enough to do His job!

Nathan did add his opinion that my Higher Meower didn't cause bad things to happen to me, but rather He'd helped me survive them. He said someday I'd understand why things happened the way they happened, which Nathan called The Vision. Until then, I needed to trust my Higher Meower and that trust was called faith.

I'd never blamed my Momcat for being a less-than-perfect mother. She did the best she could under the circumstances. She didn't have a supportive owner like The Won. (Despite his temporary lack of enthusiasm for us, I believed that one day he'd be as attentive as ever.) Candy had to go into hiding to deliver us kittens because her owner would have taken her to the Shelter upon learning she was pregnant again.

I looked around my wonderful house and I was so grateful for The Won and my family. It was true my kittenhood had been rough, but if I looked at the painful events in my life as "directive crises," they seemed less tragic and more acceptable. I always thought my life was working out great *in spite of* my early difficulties — now I realized it could very well be *because of* them. In either case, I believed my life was working out exactly the way it was supposed to.

Curled up with my dad — it still felt funny calling Bobby my dad — and Uncle Billy in the California king-size

49

bed The Won had been forced to buy to accommodate all of us, I felt at peace. The three of us were by the pillows at the head of the bed, while Nathan was curled into The Won's right side. Poor Angus, who suffered from asthma and snored terribly, slept alone at the foot of the bed.

I wondered where Candy and my sisters were at this moment. I hoped my sisters were happy and had nice homes of their own. If Candy had returned to her owner, I hoped she was being treated with kindness. When the thought occurred to me that they were all God's creatures with their own loving Higher Meower, I closed my eyes and purred.

I awoke the next day anxious to tell Flossy I couldn't see her any more. Ginger deserved my loyalty and undivided attention. I was proud of myself. Monogamy — a new value for me — was a direct result of wanting to do the right thing and please my Higher Meower. Nathan would also be pleased that I'd be spending more time at home and less time prowling the neighborhood.

Just as I was about to go out the cat door, however, The Won grabbed me and put me in the cat carrier. "Time to go see Dr. Gary," The Won said. "We can't have you prowling anymore and there's only one way I know to fix that."

Thus, I came to understand what "fixed" meant and thus ended my moral dilemma. This wasn't going to be like a vasectomy that could be reversed. What was being removed wasn't just my ability to be a father; it was my desire to pursue fatherhood. No longer would I be a heat-seeking missile; love and lust were about to become distant memories — my future role in such activities diminished to that of a consultant.

50

Chapter Seven
The Reunion

Summer and fall passed uneventfully and, although The Won wasn't himself, at least he was functional. When he could no longer ignore the imminent arrival of Christmas, he hoisted a gigantic evergreen tree in our living room and strung lights around the outer periphery of the house. Colored balls made of glass and plastic were everywhere and six stockings hung by the chimney with care — one for Nathan, Angus, Bobby, Billy, The Won and me. Christmas carols played on the radio, *Scrooge* flickered on the TV, and apple cider spiked with cloves heated on the kitchen stove.

Ever since I'd discovered my mother's identity, I'd thought about finding her and my three sisters, my family of origin. (God, how hated that term; it made us all sound like a bunch of chimpanzees.) The closer the holidays drew, the greater the urgency I felt to actually do something about finding them.

Call me a dreamer, but I yearned to experience the kind of holiday reunion that would make the last scene in "It's A Wonderful Life" pale in poignancy. It wasn't that I didn't appreciate my current family. I did. Quite frankly, I wanted both — my adopted family as well as my mother and sisters, whom I pictured as "Norman Rockwell" subjects in a "Currier and Ives" setting. I closed my eyes envisioning the "Hallmark" moment we would reunite, embracing under gently falling snowflakes that settled on our whiskers and thick coats of fur like sparkling diamonds. However, I had to find them first.

Extracting Candy's last-known address from Bobby wasn't as easy as I thought it would be, due to a reluctance on his part to give me the information. Bobby looked uncomfortable every time I mentioned my saintly mother in the glowing terms in which I remembered her. That selfless, dedicated soul was either hunting food for us, washing us or carrying us by the scruff of our necks to a warmer and safer spot in the alley. I got goose flesh when I recalled her devotion to her offspring.

Bobby gave me a peculiar look when I reminisced about Candy, but he actually said very little. However, he apparently had plenty to say to Nathan, who instigated a heart-to-heart chat with me about expectations — and specifically the advisability of having none. Candy might not want to see me, Nathan cautioned. He said seeing me might be a painful reminder of a past she'd rather forget. I listened, only giving lip service to his warning, and before you could say "Oprah Winfrey," I was out the door and on my way to a reunion with Candy who I hoped could provide some leads to the whereabouts of my sweet sisters.

I followed Bobby's advice about never traveling on an empty stomach. Remembering how he'd stuff his cheeks with kibbles to bring them to me at the top of the hill, I stored an ample supply in mine as a precaution against hunger. Looking like I had a bad case of the mumps, I was prepared to venture beyond my usual realm to the white house with black shutters that Bobby described as Candy's former residence.

I didn't like the look of the house as soon as it came into view. It was more grey than white and the yard was littered with plastic kids' toys. Two old cars were up on blocks in the

52

driveway and trash was piled around the yard. As I hid behind a fire hydrant, I saw a man wearing a torn teeshirt and a baseball cap emerge from the house. Even on The Won's worst day, he was a fashion plate compared to this specimen. I didn't want to believe he was my mother's owner, but he looked like the type who'd intimidate her into leaving home rather than risk being discovered pregnant. I took an instant dislike to this *de classe´* individual who proceeded to scratch himself, proving my point.

I could see a white plastic Christmas tree in the living room window — "how gauche," I thought, confirming my prejudice. Waiting for him to re-enter the house, I emerged from behind the hydrant and skulked up to the window. By now I was ambivalent about whether I wanted to find my mother living in this awful place or not. I stretched to peer inside the window, but as soon as I did, the blinds unfurled with a resounding crash as they hit the bottom of the window sill. "Rats!" I thought, recovering my balance and pressing my face so close to the window I flattened out my whiskers. I tried to see around the blinds, but my view was totally obstructed.

While I was peering inside, the kitchen door opened and slammed shut with a bang, and before my very eyes, staring me right in the face, appeared my sainted mother, Candy. I knew she wasn't an apparition because she spit at me — a natural reaction to finding a strange tomcat on your stoop. I didn't take offense because I realized she didn't recognize me. I barely recognized her, she'd gotten so old and wrinkled. Where were those dancing blue eyes and that nice raspy pink tongue I remembered? It was clear she'd had a hard life.

"Mom, don't you know me?" I said excitedly. "It's me, your son."

"Which son?" she asked with puzzled indifference.

I couldn't believe it! She was about as warm as a
telemarketer. Maybe she had Alzheimers, I thought, giving her
maternal instincts the benefit of the doubt. "It's me, Fred," I
insisted, before I realized that Fred was the name The Won had
given me *after* I was adopted. What had she called me?
"Here?" That sounded familiar. I tried to remember those early
days living in the alley, but I drew a blank. She probably just
called me "son," I reasoned, since I was the only male. Then
what did she call my sisters? There were three of them. The
more I tried to remember, the more confused I became. What
difference did it make anyway? Maybe she didn't need to call
us anything at all. Wasn't her mouth always full — of us?

"Remember the alley next to McDonald's?" I reminded
her. "You gave birth to me and my sisters there." I was relieved
to finally see a glint of recognition in her eyes, but horrified at
my next thought. What if my real name was "Big Mac?"

"Oh, you were part of *that* litter," she said, her voice
devoid of emotion, emphasizing the word "that." This reunion
sure wasn't the Hallmark moment I'd planned. She was
supposed to embrace me, tears of joy running down her fuzzy
cheeks, and she still hadn't made a move toward me. Perhaps
my early memories of her were wrong and she just wasn't the
demonstrative type. That would explain why her owners were
so indifferent to her. Pets were required to be affectionate.
Bobby said it was in our contract — the one the animal shelter
gave to prospective owners.

While I took Candy's inventory, she studied me. "So,
how are you?" she asked.

54

I didn't know whether to answer, "not as good as I think I am" or "better than I think I am," so I stood there dumbly. I always did think too much; Bobby said so.

"OK," she said, "Let's try a different question. How in the world did you find me?"

When I told her my connection to Bobby, she smiled in such a way it left no doubt she was having lewd thoughts of Bobby and no thoughts of me. Then she confirmed it. "That Bobby! He was something else! A great roll in the hay... but so-o-o controlling! As soon as he started telling me what to do and how to do it, I started auditioning his replacement — Stud. I didn't think he'd find out about Stud, but he did — after I'd been impregnated by both of them. Talk about lousy timing!" She sighed. "You certainly favor Stud, but you probably have a gene or two of Bobby's." Her smile faded with her memories, leaving an awkward silence which I felt compelled to fill.

"When I found out about you, I had to see you again — and my sisters. I needed to know you were all OK. I was afraid that hateful Tiger might have harmed you," I said breathless.

"Now what would make you think that ol' tom would harm me or my girls?" she asked puzzled.

She obviously suffered from long-term memory loss, but not me! I could still clearly picture fat, lazy Tiger lying around the alley, only expending energy to beat me up. I was dumbfounded she didn't remember how nasty and violent Tiger was. "Because ... because Tiger was a vicious animal; he beat me up every day!" I stammered.

55

She looked puzzled rather than disturbed. "Oh honey, you're exaggerating! He didn't beat you up. He was just playing with you." she said.

I was even more flabbergasted, but she just looked at me sadly, dismissing my version of our family history with one swish of her tail. "You *are* exaggerating, you know; it wasn't that bad," she repeated, trying to believe what she was saying.

I wanted to remind her what a "no good" Tiger was, how he just laid around and never worked, making her shoulder all the responsibility for us, but she was probably in denial about that, too. I couldn't help asking, "Why did you think I left? Why did you think I ran away at such a young age?"

"Oh, I knew you didn't get along with Tiger, but it would have been unusual if you had. Tomcats don't get along; they fight — that's what tomcats do. I knew you'd eventually have to strike out on your own, make your own mark in the world. I admit you were still a little young to leave when you did, but you always were precocious."

"So much for guilt," I thought. She obviously wasn't Jewish, so I figuratively began to bark up a different tree. "Do you know what happened to my sisters?" I asked.

"I honestly don't remember much about them," she replied, "except how attached to me they were."

Her indifference was beginning to piss me off. "Of course they were attached to you; they were still nursing," I said sarcastically.

"Oh yes," she continued, deflecting my comment like Wonder Woman deflecting bullets with her magic bracelets. "Let me think. It seems to me I heard they were all adopted by one family — live somewhere off of Lorcum Lane. But that was a while ago."

I brightened; Lorcum Lane wasn't far from home, *my* home and *my* family. It might take some time to find them, but I knew I could if I looked long and hard enough. Three female cats living in the same household was unusual enough for other creatures to notice and I'd ask around.

While I planned ahead, Candy stretched her long limbs. "Don't you think I still look pretty good for my age?" she purred.

"Oh my God," I thought, "I hope she isn't flirting with me. Who does she think I am, anyway, Oedipus Rex?" I was glad I'd eaten all the kibbles I'd stored in my cheeks while I staked out the house from behind the fire hydrant. Otherwise I surely would have choked on them. "I really have to be going now," I said blushing. "It was nice to see you, though, and I'll try to come back again." I added, even though I had no intention of returning — which was always the case when I said I'd "try" to do something.

"I hope so, Fred," she said, looking back at me as she returned to her run-down house.

As I left, I took my emotional temperature. I was surprised I wasn't more disappointed because this reunion fell far short of my dreams. I thought of the expression, "when your dreams turn to dust, vacuum," and smiled. God knows, I had enough experience feeling sorry for myself, but for some reason I didn't this time. Perhaps I'd finally learned to wear life like a loose garment.

I was grateful instead of sad. What's more, I was feeling these feelings in real time for a change. Usually it was weeks before I connected my feelings to the event that provoked them. I realized how lucky I was to have Nathan, Bobby, Billy, Angus and The Won. They were my *real* family, the ones who loved me and worried about my well being. Nathan always told me to be grateful for what I had instead of regretting what I didn't have. I was.

I never felt luckier, considering where I came from. I was null and void until Nathan and Bobby introduced me to my "self." I now realize that I didn't have a chance of developing self-esteem until I discovered that self. At first I balked at some of their suggestions, until it occurred to me that Nathan and Bobby never asked me to do anything they weren't already doing themselves. They didn't tell me how to live; they showed me how to live. And by doing exactly as they did, I was becoming as happily and usefully whole as they were.

As I trotted home, I thought about each member of my "real" family. Angus, the little dweeb, followed The Won everywhere he went: down to the front of the house when The Won washed his car or patched the retaining wall with plaster; to the backyard where The Won repainted the deck and mowed the hills; and to the side of the yard to straighten the fence that acted as a barrier between us and our neighbors, Arsenic and Old Lace. The Won earned his naps while Angus' exhaustion was vicarious.

I thought about my Uncle Billy. (It still seemed funny calling him Uncle Billy.) He was a paradox — an intellectual who had the least to say about anything. You'd never know how smart he was unless you asked him about stuff. He never volunteered information and was very shy, still spending a lot of time in the back closet — probably thinking. But every once in awhile he'd bust loose and chase Bobby like he did when they were kittens. They'd race through the house like a tornado, upsetting lamps, vases and everything else in their path.

I loved the fact that Bobby was one of my fathers. It excused all the unwanted advice he tried to give me when I first arrived. In-Your-Face-Bobby I called him. He was always there, especially when you wished he weren't.

As for Nathan, he was all-wise and wonderful, encouraging me, teaching me, and answering my questions. I loved Nathan and hated to see him limping in pain or watch his whiskers getting whiter and thinner. I hated the thought of him getting old and fat, losing his memory and his fur.

Ditto for The Won. It was true I didn't have much of a relationship with The Won any more, but Nathan said not to worry. The Won would eventually snap out of his depression, and, by that time, I'd be mature and experienced enough to relate to him on a much more sophisticated level. I didn't want our relationship to be so sophisticated I couldn't sleep with him or sit on his lap, because he gave good body heat.

I hadn't slackened my pace for a minute, and my reward was that I could now smell my neighborhood. As I rounded the corner, I cut through Arsenic and Old Lace's backyard and headed for my cat door. I couldn't wait to be home, my home.

Chapter Eight
A Hare Power

Sitting in the den, waiting for Nathan and Bobby to join me for our daily meeting, I stared at the picture of Nathan and BR on the wall. It was easy to see how symbiotic their relationship was by the kindness and love that shone in BR's eyes and the intensity with which Nathan was listening to him. Although you could only see Nathan's back in the photo, you could tell how intent he was by the way his head was cocked.

Staying in the house when the weather was bad always gave me a case of cabin fever, and I'd already been under involuntary confinement for nearly four days due to a current rash of ice storms. I couldn't imagine how BR stayed sane, much less happy, in that claustrophobic, small cage. I would have gone stark raving mad if I were similarly confined. (Come to think of it, that's probably what drove the "Mad Hatter" mad.) There was nothing more precious than freedom, I mused, as I hummed a few bars of "My Country T'is of Thee."

There was so much I wanted to know about BR. Maybe he had a lot of hobbies to keep him busy. Did his family visit him? I knew he had relatives — Brer Rabbit, Frere Rabbit and a lot of cousins on the Hare side of the family. (I'd heard that Mere and Pere Rabbit died prematurely as a result of some diabolical scientific experiments — pregnancy tests.)

There were also things I wanted to know about Nathan, questions I'd been meaning to ask when we were alone; however, these days we never seemed to be alone. Nathan was getting old and I didn't want him to die before I learned as much about him and BR as I could. I wanted Nathan's perspective on life, his history, because I knew it would be rich and there would be much I could learn from it.

When Nathan entered the den, he said, "Bobby can't make it this afternoon; The Won is taking him to Dr. Gary for his rabies shots. So it's just you and me, kid." Coincidence? I think not. Nathan slowly squatted down next to me. I could tell raising and lowering himself was a painful process. When I asked him what was causing his pain, he laughed.

"When you're young, Fred, there usually is a cause for pain, but when you're old *that* is the cause."

I felt badly for Nathan (and worse for Bobby who was off to the vet), but I was glad we'd have this opportunity to talk. "I was just looking at the picture of you and BR," I said. "Was BR always in that awful cage? Why did he have to stay in there? Were his owners afraid he'd run away?" I shot one question after another at Nathan, rapid-fire, until my words stumbled over each other.

Nathan smiled. "You wouldn't be trying to avoid today's lesson, would you?" He suspected an ulterior motive.

"I'm not, honest, Nathan," I replied. For the past few days we'd been discussing each of the seven deadly sins and today's lesson on sloth was a subject to which I couldn't relate. "I've examined my conscience," I said sincerely, "and I don't have a problem with sloth. I'm not old enough to think about retiring," I added, "so can we talk about something else?"

My words unleashed a tirade from Nathan. "Despite what some books may say, Fred, sloth is not synonymous with retiring. As a matter of fact, I don't know anyone who's retired who has the time or luxury to be slothful these days. The definition of sloth is lethargy, indolence, and laziness. It has nothing to do with retirement."

I'd obviously touched a nerve. "So can we talk about BR instead?" I quickly asked, changing the subject. Nathan looked up at the picture of BR and his face softened.

"Sure, Fred," I could tell he was tired by the way he agreed so readily. "What do you want to know?"

"Tell me how you first met BR?" I asked. "Was he always a prisoner? Was he always fat?" (I admit I was tactless.) "Or did you first meet him when he was a young, fair hare, a slender offender?"

"Slow down Fred. Why don't I start from the beginning," Nathan said, clearing his throat. "I met BR quite by accident," Nathan continued. "I was out in the neighborhood one day and I noticed this cage in the driveway next door. I went over to investigate and there was BR, sitting inside chewing on some carrots. He was huge even then, and so unusual looking that he sparked my curiosity. I thought he looked like 'Jabba the Hut' from *Star Wars*."

I was pretty lonesome — I was an "only cat" at the time — and I didn't get along very well with the neighborhood cats because I considered them competition. I always felt different and alone. The best way I can describe how I felt is "an anxious apartness." I never had anyone to talk to, so you could say that I started visiting BR out of a sense of quiet desperation. I wasn't very happy back then. I was restless, irritable and discontented, even though I had no reason to be. The Won was a pretty stand-up guy and there really wasn't anything wrong with my life except my perception of it. At any rate, BR was a captive audience and I thought he might be lonesome too, so I started telling him about myself. Well, actually I started making up fantastic stories about myself, which BR saw right through." Nathan smiled at the memory.

"Whenever I felt offended by life, I'd visit BR and talk to him until I was hoarse. He was pretty quiet at first, but after awhile he started giving me advice. I remember the day I fell and failed to land on my feet. I was mortified because some of the neighborhood cats had been watching and I knew they were all laughing at me behind my back. When I told BR about it, he gave me my first lesson in humility. He told me, 'You wouldn't care so much what others thought of you, if you realized how seldom they did.'"

"On another occasion when BR accidentally tipped his cage over, I tried to be a hero and right it single-handedly, particularly after a small crowd of those same cats gathered as onlookers at the scene of the accident. Here was a chance to prove myself. BR watched me sweat and strain for quite awhile — I thought I was going to have a hernia —until he insisted I ask for help from the others. I didn't want to, because I knew they were judging me and would think me a weakling, but I did. When we righted the cage, it felt good being a part of something greater than myself, a team effort, instead of always being so self-reliant. I found out those other cats really liked me. They were never judging me; it was all in my head."

63

"Before I knew it, spending time with BR became the highlight of my day." Nathan continued with enthusiasm. "I really cared about BR. He was my closest friend, my family. I trusted BR like no other — except The Won, of course, but that was a different kind of trust. I trusted BR so much, I even listened to him when he talked about spirituality and my need to find a universal source of goodness in my life.

"BR helped me define my Higher Meower by telling me I could give it any characteristics I wanted. BR's 'Hare Power,' for example, was a cross between Bugs Bunny and the Easter Bunny. It had Bugs' looks, sense of humor and craftiness, and the Easter Bunny's unconditional love and generosity. My Higher Meower or God became all those things and more."

Nathan continued. "Once I was comfortable with a concept of God, BR taught me how to pray and meditate. He said we pray to God to make ourselves aware of Him, not to make Him aware of us. (God already knows everything about us.) And we clear our minds and meditate in order to listen to Him, often through others. BR said it was necessary to be still in order to hear God because God never shouts or competes for our attention. 'Be still and know that I am God' was one of BR's favorite psalms," Nathan said.

"BR taught me everything I know about faith, the belief that God's will (the way things work out) is always in my best interest. Until I had faith in my Higher Meower, I mistakenly believed that others caused things to happen or kept things from happening. BR taught me about leading a rich, happy, spiritual life and maintaining healthy relationships with family, friends, and significant others. He awakened the dormant spirit within me by teaching me twelve principles by which to live:

64

honesty, hope, faith, integrity, courage, willingness, humility, love, justice, perseverance, spirituality and generosity."

I'd never witnessed Nathan so passionate. He was so eloquent, his speech brought tears to his eyes.

Nathan looked thoughtful for a moment, then a little sad. "I visited BR almost every day, but I was so self-centered I never thought to ask him about himself or why he was locked up in that cage. I just accepted that it was his role in life to be my personal advisor and always accessible when I needed him. BR was there for my convenience, so I never questioned what he wanted out of life or whether he had any dreams of his own. It wasn't until after he died that I found out he was actually incarcerated for sex offenses with no possibility of parole.

I'm sure Nathan told me this so I could see what a study in acceptance BR was, but, instead of satisfying my curiosity, it prompted even more questions. "Are all bunny rabbits sex offenders? Did he get a fair trial? Did they have pictures or other hard evidence to convict him? Do all rabbits have to spend their lives in cages? Did BR's owners get another rabbit after BR died?" I asked. There was so much I wanted to know.

Nathan said he honestly didn't have the answers to my questions, and he'd never tried to learn more about BR or rabbits in general after BR died. It was too painful; the mere mention of the species sent him into despair. He was so heartbroken, he couldn't bring himself to think about rabbits ever again, even during Easter. His only consolation for BR's premature death came from BR himself. "He must have known he was dying when he told me, 'Life shouldn't be measured by its length, but rather by its depth,'" Nathan said.

When I looked at the clock, I was surprised to see that our hour together had already passed. I had a lot to think about. It must have been awful when Nathan was by himself; I was glad I'd never been an only cat. When Nathan was talking about BR, he had the same sad look in his eyes that I now saw in The Won's. So that was what grief looked like. But if Nathan could get over his, I was sure The Won would, too. Nathan said The Won would have to do that himself because we'd proven that we couldn't fix him.

Trying to bring interesting animals home to distract The Won certainly hadn't worked. My heart had been in the right place, but The Won was human after all, unpredictable and not the best candidate for my newly-acquired compassion and logical thinking.

Perhaps I needed to let go of The Won, I thought. There were plenty of other creatures out there who needed my help and who would be more responsive. Almost every lesson I'd learned from Nathan and Bobby had the same moral theme, i.e. to feel better about myself, help others. So I decided to track down someone to help whether they wanted my help or not. I combed the neighborhood looking for a creature to help with the same selfless dedication and determination of a Buddhist Monk searching for the next Dahli Lama.

As I walked up and down the hills from one *cul de sac* to another, I thought about how glad I was Nathan told me about BR and their relationship. I wondered why I'd never asked him about himself before. It just hadn't occurred to me. I wondered if Nathan would ever have volunteered such intimate information about himself. Probably not, I thought. The older generation was pretty tight-lipped about discussing their feelings because they'd been taught being vulnerable was synonymous with being weak. You never talked about how you felt. You didn't air your dirty laundry in public. Children were seen and not heard. Boy, was I glad times had changed.

After scouring the neighborhood for an hour, the only creature I'd seen was Angus' friend, that pesky squirrel who was beyond help. I looked up at the sun. It was close to noon, equivalent to midnight in cat time. All my friends who were also nocturnally inclined were undoubtedly taking afternoon naps by now, which sounded like an excellent idea to me. Then, like a bolt out of the blue, I was the recipient of divine inspiration. Maybe my sisters needed help. Now I had another reason to find them!

Chapter Nine
Candy and My Sweet Sisters

I'd had a nagging, uncomfortable feeling in the pit of my stomach ever since I'd visited Candy and harbored less than charitable thoughts about her — resentful thoughts directly related to her revisionist history of the animal abuse I suffered as a kitten. Although I could justify my ill feelings, I didn't like having them. I'd learned a very important spiritual axiom from Nathan and Bobby: "Every time I was disturbed, no matter what the cause, there was something wrong with me." I knew I had to come to terms with my past to be at peace in the present.

Why hadn't I looked for my sisters earlier? Was I afraid they'd confirm Candy's version of our history? Was I hoping they really needed my help — needed me to rescue them? Was I selfishly hoping that while I'd always landed on my feet, they'd be up to their ears in litter?

I always considered my conscience clear until I heard Nathan say: "Those who have a clear conscience usually have a poor memory." Did I always treat my sisters with love and respect? Did I do all I could to keep them out of harm's way. Finding them and facing my fears would take me out of my emotional comfort zone, but I knew I must. "The only way you build muscle is by picking up weights that are too heavy for you, and the only way you build character is by facing situations that are too uncomfortable to ignore," Bobby said.

When I retreated to that spot within myself where I stood totally naked (or fur-less, in my case) to meet my Higher

Meower, I had to admit I was afraid of what I might discover. What if I didn't feel anything toward my sisters? What if I did? What if I didn't like them? What if they didn't like me? I knew the only way out of this emotional quagmire was to take action. I could pray that when I finally did meet my sisters, the God in me would talk to the God in them.

Once I made up my mind to begin the search, I had to tell someone. I was more bull-headed than most, but Nathan had drilled the lesson into my head that when I was about to embark on a venture in which I had a lot of emotion invested, it was best to run it by someone who was more objective. Since Bobby had been involved with Candy and was the father of my sisters, he didn't qualify as "objective." Yet, I knew he deserved to be told what I was about to do. So I announced my decision to find my sisters to both he and Nathan at the same time, during our next meeting in the den.

I spent the hour before our meeting rehearsing what I would say, what Bobby would say, then what I would say in response to what he said. Even as I was carrying on this conversation in my head, I knew I was violating one of Nathan's most sacred tenets: "Keep your head where your feet are planted and only talk to those who are present." Because I was uncomfortable confronting family issues, I was sure Bobby would feel the same, telling me to leave well enough alone and forget about my sisters. However, much to my amazement, his reaction was exactly the opposite. I underestimated him.

I was guilty of being overly dramatic, as usual. It was a family joke. If one of the others missed a meal, they'd call The Won to feed them. If I missed a meal, I'd call 911. Bobby was not only supportive, he was actually helpful, suggesting I start

69

my inquiries about the girls with the big black female Labrador Retriever who lived over on 35th Street. Her owner was a jogger who took her on extended runs, so she ventured the furthest afield from our neighborhood than any other creature. She had a reputation for keeping her nose to the ground and would be an invaluable source of intelligence about Lorcum Lane. The only other advice I received was from Nathan, who told me to make sure I brought my Higher Meower with me.

I didn't need to be reminded of that. My Higher Meower was my invisible best friend, my celestial superman, my supreme intelligence and my bountiful benefactor, all rolled into one. I looked upon all my travels as "Fred and HM's Excellent Adventures."

I walked over to the sliding glass door in the dining room where The Won was seated at the table. This was an important moment in my life. I felt that the start of such a noble mission should be marked by as dignified an exit as possible; so I wanted to leave through a real door rather than by ducking through our cat door. I stood tall in front of the sliding glass patio door, stared at the handle for awhile, meowed, then looked directly at The Won to see if he was getting the message. He knew what I wanted and was either so apathetic he didn't care if I used my own door, or truly sensitive to the importance of the mission on which I was about to embark. In any case, he stood up and opened the dining room door with a flourish.

I stood halfway in and halfway out of the opened door as the cold air rushed into the house. Standing in open doorways was where I did some of my best thinking, particularly when the weather was most inclement. Before I had a chance to gather my thoughts, however, The Won gently encouraged me to leave with the help of his foot. As I exited the house on the end of it, the words "stand tall and never let anyone diminish your worth" rang in my ears. Anxious to begin my journey, I bounded out the door, over the deck, around the house and down the retaining wall to the street. As I set out from our *cul de sac*, I was absolutely certain I was on the right path — because it was going uphill.

I did question the black Lab, as well as several other creatures with whom I had a nodding acquaintance, en route to Lorcom Lane. It would have been impossible to locate my sisters had they been indoor cats, but fortunately they weren't. They shared my love of the great outdoors and were regularly seen around their neighborhood, displaying the same zest for life as me. Despite being cold outside, it was bright and sunny, so chances were good that they'd be out. As soon as I got within range of their neighborhood, I kept a sharp eye peeled for a girl who looked like me and one or two others who looked like Bobby.

I saw my "identical twin" first. She was half way up a tree, although I couldn't tell if she was on her way up or down. When I walked to the base of the tree and hollered at her, she descended so fast it was hard to gauge her intentions. But when I told her who I was, she jumped right on top of me and began slobbering all over me. (I liked the kid's enthusiasm.) And by the time I picked myself up from the ground, I was surrounded by two more females — blondes. The whole family was here!

My two blonde sisters knew who I was immediately without being told (so much for derisive comments about "dumb" blondes). It was such an emotional moment, it seemed

71

odd to have to introduce ourselves, but none of us had names when we were last together, only colors. My twin was now called Oreo; our sisters were Caramel and Butterscotch. (Although their names were derivative of "candy," the human who named the girls couldn't have known that Candy was our mother's name, so he or she obviously had a major issue with food.) Despite the blondes having identical markings, they were easy to tell apart because Butterscotch was a plus size — definitely her father's daughter. (If he'd needed clothes, Bobby would have been a regular customer of *Big and Tall*, and he could hardly be considered tall.)

The girls and I were so excited to be together, we spent the afternoon chasing each other, wrestling, and climbing trees. By the time we stopped to rest in a sunny spot on the lawn, we were all panting. "Gee, it sure is good to see you, Fred," Oreo purred. "I want to know everything about you. Where do you live? Are you near here? Do you have nice owners? Are you an only pet? Do you like your humans?" She sounded just like me.

It was clear the girls never had to fend for themselves by their assumption that I had owners who took care of me and that I lived in a nice home like theirs. They'd gone right from the protection of our Momcat to the protection of an owner. Not only didn't they need any help from me, but they had more than me. I felt a small resentment bubbling up because they'd also never suffered the hardships that I had to endure.

It was tempting to tell them how I sacrificed my well-being for theirs, how I left to prevent their possibly bearing the brunt of misdirected hatred Tiger felt toward me. The truth was melodramatic enough, but after embellishing it a bit they'd weep unabashedly and beg me to let them make it up to me. I would tell them the whole story at some appropriate time, but not now, I thought charitably.

It was apparent my sisters shared Candy's view of why I left home, and that was OK for now. I did tell them something about my travels, which I made sound adventurous rather than the desperate and frightening experiences they were. When I got to the part about being adopted by The Won and living with Nathan and the others, the girls smiled with delight. When I added my discovery that Bobby was actually one of our fathers and told them I'd visited Candy, our mother, they squealed with excitement and could hardly contain themselves.

I didn't want to taint their fond recollections of our family life, so I'd refrained from saying anything derogatory about Tiger, but when my sisters kept referring to him like he was a saint, it really twisted my tail. When I couldn't stand it any longer, I finally interrupted. "Wait just a minute," I said, incapable of hearing one more accolade about my nemesis. "He was despicable! Don't you remember how he used to beat me?" I asked, amazed they didn't recall anything unkind about him.

Caramel spoke up first. "It's true Tiger wasn't very nice to you, Fred, but that was partly your fault. You challenged him at every turn and broke all of his rules, and when he tried to get close to Mom, you'd come between them and get right in Tiger's face. When he batted you away, he tried to be gentle, but you'd keep coming back for more until you were physically exhausted. And when Mom wasn't around, you peed right where Tiger slept — on purpose."

Oreo piped in, "You sure made him mad, Fred! It was probably a good thing you left when you did; otherwise, Tiger might *really* have hurt you. You were both so stubborn! Mom used to say so all the time, even when she was trying to protect you. When you left, Fred, Mom was heartbroken. She looked all over for you and cried herself to sleep every night for the longest time. But she knew you had to leave eventually, so she finally accepted it."

I was stunned! Three creatures — Candy, Caramel, and Oreo — had now contradicted my recollections of Tiger, volunteering an entirely different view of my "mistreatment." Nathan always told me that if three creatures who really cared about me offered me the same opinion or advice, I should accept it. But how could I give up my memories of being brutalized so easily? They were such a big part of who I was.

Butterscotch emitted a small sigh. "After we were weaned, it was Tiger who took us to the animal shelter while Mom was out hunting for food. He knew she'd never be able to part with us voluntarily, so one day he waited until she left before leading us to the steps of that shelter. He told us how hard it was for him to leave us there, while he posed us just so on the steps. Before he left, he licked each of us on the head and wished us luck. And boy were we ever lucky! That same day a nice woman came in who'd lost both of her cats within days of each other. When she was told the three of us were related and available, she decided to adopt all of us." (I didn't tell Butterscotch that luck had nothing to do with it.)

"We really want you to meet our humans, Fred. Can you come home with us?" Oreo pleaded.

All of a sudden I felt very homesick. It had been a long day. The sun was setting and I needed to be surrounded by my own things and the familiar fuzzy faces that I loved, while I digested this new truth — like most creatures, Tiger was apparently both good and bad. I had to stop seeing things as black or white and recognize that most situations were gray. I also realized that some things about Tiger, like the fact he laid around the alley all day and didn't work, were none of my business. That had been Candy's business, not mine. "No, girls, I can't stay. I need to get home, but now that I've found you, I'll come again." And I knew I would, because I didn't qualify my intentions by saying I'd "try" to come again. I didn't have time to say anything else before they began squealing with excitement, like Elvis had just walked in. I was forced to cover my ears with my paws while they covered my face with cat kisses.

When I got home I told everyone about visiting my sisters, but Angus was more concerned with his scratching post than with my late-breaking news and Billy was preoccupied chasing a fly. Nathan was delighted for me but volunteered that I owed Candy an amends when I repeated what the girls told me about Tiger. It wasn't that I'd said or done anything hurtful to Candy; I just hadn't treated her with the respect she was due as my mother. My sin was one of omission rather than commission, and Nathan reminded me that feeling uncomfortable about Candy was reason enough to make an amends because "we make amends for our own peace of mind, not anyone else's."

Bobby just bobbed his head in the affirmative, like one of those plastic dogs humans put on the dashboards of their cars. Speaking of amends, I hoped I hadn't inadvertently offended Bobby when I described Butterscotch in expansive terms, adding that she looked just like him, but it was true.

Following the directions I'd been given, I went back to visit Candy a few days later and found her lying in her driveway. It was cold and I wondered why she was outside, instead of inside curled up in a warm afghan. She looked at me curiously, then smiled. "I didn't think I'd be seeing you again," she observed. I climbed over a tricycle to get close to her.

"I found my sisters," I said proudly as I sat down. "Bobby helped me by giving me some suggestions. Their names are Oreo, Caramel and Butterscotch, and they live on Lorcum Lane at the corner of Military Road. They're well taken care of and seem happy; I thought you'd want to know." I spoke quickly without pausing to take a breath, because I didn't want to risk an uncomfortable silence.

Candy smiled. "I'm glad they're happy. You were my last litter, you know." It was a statement not a question. "Or did I tell you that the last time you were here?" I shook my head no and she continued.

"Yes, times sure have changed — and not necessarily for the better. When I was young, humans expected us to have litters, which were a natural consequence of our most basic instincts. Having kittens was a physiological fact of life, not a moral issue. We bred, we fed, then we fled — to the next tom. That was the natural order of things. It wasn't an easy life and some of us got old before our time, but we knew what was expected of us. Then those do-gooders from the SPCA and the Humane Society came around with their radical ideas. They put pressure on humans to get us fixed, saying there were too many of us in this world! Can you imagine!!!" Candy was clearly outraged by what she considered a major social injustice.

"In the end, I couldn't even let my owner know when I became pregnant with you and your sisters. So I ran away and had you secretly. It wasn't long after I returned home that my human finally buckled under the social pressure and had me fixed. I became another eunuch, fighting not for territory or honor any longer, but fighting out of sexual frustration. When I lost my right to motherhood, I lost my identity. It's been tough, Fred, but I have a new identity today, a new purpose in life."

I sat next to my mother, my mouth opened in awe. I never suspected that she was so intelligent, honest and forthright, or that she herself might have "issues." I was beginning to see her, not as my mother, but as another cat. I had compassion and a new respect for her.

"I knew I had to do something to restore my sanity and my sense of self-worth," she continued, "so I became a felinist, advocating safe sex instead of no sex at all. And I certainly have my work cut out for me, even today. But I have lots of support."

And just as Candy finished talking, a stream of cats walked up her driveway. "Here comes my support group now," she said as she greeted them by name. "Hi, Fluffy, Princess Di, Midnight, Lisa, Pearl, Frankie, ..." The names went on and on. "You're welcome to stay for our meeting, Fred," she offered.

"I really can't," I replied hastily, wondering if she'd joined a cult or, worse yet, if she was its leader. "But I'll come back tomorrow when you're not so busy."

"Hey, everyone; this is my boy Fred!" Candy shouted the general introduction with pride, while I scanned their faces.

I knew I had nothing to fear from this group; they all seemed decent enough — not a degenerate in the lot, I concluded. As Candy licked my head, I thought of how long I'd been waiting for that sign of love and approval from her. Then I remembered what Nathan said: "It's never too late to have a happy kittenhood." I smiled as I looked at Candy. It was also never too late to be a good parent, I thought.

Chapter Ten
Run Rabbit, Run!

I always *felt* different — probably because I *was* different. Unlike other cats who stayed close to home after being neutered, the procedure only affected my lust, not my wanderlust. I loved to travel and used any excuse to take a trip, including the fact it was a holiday. Normally, human holidays didn't mean much to me, but Easter, only a week away, had special significance. While I paid scant attention to its religious overtones, it was a very spiritual holiday for me because of its association with rabbits. In view of BR's legacy to Nathan, Nathan's to Bobby, and both of theirs to me, any holiday that revered rabbits was worthy of celebration. So I planned to do what countless others did during holidays — visit my mother.

My decision to visit Candy was so mature, I knew I was finally developing real values, and those values had nothing to do with power, property or prestige. It was true that I lived in a fine house with plenty of toys, but I didn't consider any of those things really mine. The way I looked at it, they didn't actually belong to me; I only had temporary use of them. Where material things were concerned, I *always* minimized their importance, even when I was young and resented not having them. I wondered if I'd think material possessions were so irrelevant today if I was still devoid of them.

It was clear poor Candy started with nothing — and had managed to hang on to most of it. I wanted more for her, but she seemed content living in relative poverty. Maybe, like the Sisters of the Poor, she truly had everything she needed.

Certainly she seemed to treasure her health and her freedom the most. We were alike in that respect; I also appreciated my ability to come and go as I pleased, and wished my brothers could say the same.

Poor Nathan was limited by his arthritis and had to be content staying inside, watching *GO CAT* videos; Angus, who had asthma, couldn't go out all spring because of the pollen in the air; Billy, who was afraid of his own shadow, was restricted to the yard by his fear; Bobby, who only refused food when he misunderstood the question, was hampered in getting around by his weight; and The Won, who was still depressed, had lost his passion for travel and adventure. So I felt tremendously lucky in comparison.

We were quite a group! Thank goodness we could laugh at ourselves and each other, which we often did. However, we wisely drew the line at laughing at each other's expense. In the Clarke family, we never shot our wounded; otherwise, we'd all be dead. Instead, we trained to be better soldiers.

We were an odd little family and compared ourselves to a football team that drew strength and encouragement from each other in the huddle. We'd circle, paws on each other's shoulders, chanting, "We are bodily and mentally different from our fellows. Hike!" before going out into the world for another play, only to return to the huddle for additional support, chanting, "We are bodily and mentally different from our fellows. Hike!"

It was rare that we all enjoyed mental health on the same day, so we tried to help whoever needed it the most as best we could. Nathan and Bobby's tutoring was a good example of the preemptive help they gave me to deal with potential problems and life in general. I just wished I had someone to whom I could pass on the valuable "life lessons" I was learning.

It was hard for me to believe I was the same kitten who'd come to them, trampled by the hideous Four Horsemen: Terror, Bewilderment, Frustration, and Despair. Today my emotional lows weren't nearly as dramatic. I was hardly ever bewildered by events or felt the extremes of terror and despair. True, I was still sad and afraid occasionally, but the severity of my feelings had been tempered by my ability to first identify them, and then pray to my Higher Meower for their removal.

When I was a kitten, I looked at feelings like enemy missiles. I'd issue a feelings alert as soon as I sensed an incoming and try to stop or divert it before it reached me. When I wasn't successful, I was often suicidal. Then I'd get angry and think, "Why kill myself when there are others?" Come to think of it, I was always either angry, resentful or fearful. It was Nathan who explained that all three emotions were related and stemmed from the same self-centered fear. Anger was a result of not getting what I wanted today. Resentment was a result of not getting what I wanted yesterday, and fear was a result of thinking I wouldn't get what I wanted tomorrow.

Where fear was concerned, I'd start by projecting death, then work backwards to being alone, helpless and hopeless, no matter what the immediate cause . . . getting lost, misplacing something valuable, missing a meal, etc. However, when I recognized the fear for what it was, I could deal with it by

81

reminding myself that I was part of a family and never had to be alone again, and that my Higher Meower was always taking care of me, regardless of my circumstances and especially when my life wasn't going the way I thought it should.

I remembered when Nathan and Bobby first started talking to me about believing in God or a Higher Meower. I was skeptical, to say the least. Finally Nathan said, "If you can't believe, at least believe that I believe." That seemed simple enough.

It was Bobby who suggested that I could use anything as a higher power, even a door knob. When I asked why a door knob, he said because it would eventually open the door to a stronger spiritual belief as long as I remained teachable. Finally, Nathan said the only thing I really needed to believe was that everything was going to be all right. I could relate to that because I honestly felt better when I thought a loving Higher Meower was out there somewhere, even though I wasn't 100% convinced. Bobby said that even if I didn't believe in God, God still believed in me.

When I felt frustrated that I didn't "understand" God, Bobby reminded me that I never would, because God was infinite (immeasurable and without limits), while I was finite (definitely limited in capacity). He said that rather than trying to understand God, I should concentrate my energy on forming a relationship with Him — and that meant communicating with Him every day through prayer and meditation.

Nathan taught me that I shouldn't pray for "things," so I prayed for happiness instead. I asked my Higher Meower *to make me* happy, but, as time went on, I realized He couldn't *make me* happy without my cooperation. So I altered my prayer to *let me* be happy, hoping He'd remove any obstacles to getting the things I needed in order to be happy. After awhile I realized that "things" were never going to make me happy, so I asked Him to *show me* how to be happy. I finally understood that I was responsible for my own happiness and that happiness was the inner peace which resulted from my allegiance with Him and my fellows.

I skipped along to Candy's house feeling truly grateful. Having a second family to love was better than rolling around in Atomic Catnip. My life was like an equilateral triangle. At the top was my home with The Won and my brothers. At the bottom right was Candy and at the bottom left were my sisters, Oreo, Caramel and Butterscotch. I saw that triangle encircled by my loving Higher Meower who was taking care of us all. I felt so spiritual I thought I might levitate!

When I arrived at Candy's, we decided to go for a long walk. It was a perfect spring day. All the azaleas and daffodils were in bloom, and when a breeze blew through the flowering dogwood trees, beautiful white and pink petals gently drifted to the ground like new-fallen snow. As we walked though the petals, I told Candy about BR and the significance Easter held for me. I knew she'd be moved by the story, but I didn't expect her to totally break down. When I questioned why she was sobbing uncontrollably, instead of telling me, she showed me.

Leading me across the street and into the backyard of a neighbor, Candy approached a large tarp-covered box at the end of the driveway. Taking the cover in her teeth, she tugged at the tarp until it fell to the ground, revealing a cage that looked strangely familiar. What I saw amazed me because there

before my very eyes were five miniature versions of BR —
tiny, white, fluffy bunnies with long pink ears, twitching noses
and little cotton tails — hopping around a straw-covered cage
similar to the one pictured in our den. "Why these are rabbits!"
I exclaimed, using my astute powers of observation. "How
wonderful! Little br's!" My joy blinded me from seeing their
true circumstances, proving the adage: "We don't see things the
way *they* are; we see things the way *we* are."

Candy sobbed even louder. She said I didn't understand. She explained that these rabbits were for sale by humans
who bought them as pets for their small children at Easter time.
Unfortunately, children, by their very nature, were easily bored
and too immature to take care of them. So after a couple of
months, the rabbits would end up at the animal shelter to be put
to death. And those were the lucky ones! The ones that
remained unsold by Easter sometimes ended up in stew pots.

Candy felt horrible because, although she'd been long
aware of this practice, she'd never done anything about it.
She'd never known any rabbits personally, so she'd always
looked the other way, rationalizing that it was none of her
business. After hearing about BR, however, she could no
longer ignore this barbarism. She told me the mark of
immaturity was to die nobly for a cause, while the mark of
maturity was to live humbly for one. So instead of doing
something foolish to protest the rabbits' fate, like self-
immolation, we would do something positive to change their
fate.

My reaction was immediate. I, too, was appalled by the
bunnies' plight. "This is terrible!" I cried. "Talk about ethnic
cleansing! It's indecent! How could anyone kill these adorable

84

creatures? They're almost as cute as kittens!" I railed. "If we allow this genocide to continue, who knows, kittens might be next! We have to do something to save these bunnies!" (I was quite the orator when I found a worthy cause.)

Candy was delighted by my strong support and, as a feline activist, she'd already formed a plan to rectify this social injustice despite the fact that it was technically none of our business. Because this crime was being perpetrated on another species, we could have pussy-footed around, but taking action immediately was the right thing to do. Wiping away her tears, Candy said with conviction, "Let's stage a break out!"

I was so proud of my mother, I nearly burst. As I watched the five little white bunnies hopping around their cage, I knew releasing them was their only hope. "I think I can open the cage," I offered, "then all we have to do is coax them out. I just hope they can survive in the wild. They look so fragile!"

"They'll be fine," Candy said optimistically. "There are lots of wild rabbits around here and they thrive, eating grass, vegetables and flower bulbs. We don't have to worry about them freezing to death either, now that it's spring."

"What about predators?" I asked.

Candy thought for a minute. "Dogs are supposed to be leashed and other cats won't bother them — we're too sophisticated. Sure, there are opossums and racoons, but most of them are vegetarians. Besides, what do these bunnies have to lose? If we leave them here, they face certain death," she said, while I picked at the latch on the cage door.

It didn't take long to get the door open and for Candy to coax the baby bunnies out, but just as the last one, a little runt with failing eyesight, left the cage, the back door of the house swung open and a human stepped out. When he saw all five bunnies out of their cage, he let out a bellow loud enough to awaken the dead. My adrenalin was already racing with the excitement of the break out. Now it was in overdrive, given the added element of fear. My tail was on fire! Bobby said that when your tail was on fire, it was important to examine whether it was a result of self-immolation, arson or natural combustion. In this case, I'd ignited it myself, but a cat had to do what a cat had to do.

"Marge," the man hollered. "Come quick. The rabbits are loose!"

Candy and I stampeded the bunnies towards the woods, making sure they stayed in front of us. My heart was in my throat. Fortunately, the human was fat and slow and, by the time he reached the end of the driveway, Candy had already driven most of the bunnies into the underbrush towards freedom.

"Run, bunnies, run!" I screamed as I watched them hop into the woods, chased by the fat man who was zeroing in on the runt.

Sorely lagging behind, the tiny bunny was scared out of its mind and either blind as a bat or very confused, because it kept hopping in circles. When the man was within reach and stooped to grab the bunny by the ears, I threw myself on the fat man's back, claws extended. He howled in pain, then stood up, reaching behind him to pull me off, but I'd already leapt to the ground. Candy and the other four bunnies were out of sight, but the runt was still frantically hopping in circles. So I grabbed him in my mouth by the scruff of the neck and took off lickety split into the woods. I never looked back. It was amazing how justified anger fueled my speed and stamina!

After awhile, I had to rest. It was hard to pant while I had a rabbit in my mouth, so I gently laid the terrified creature down in a patch of sweet-smelling grass. I told him that Candy and I had rescued him and his siblings for their own good, that if they'd stayed in that cage they'd surely die, but the bunny just looked at me — a little stupidly, if you want to know the truth. He was probably still in shock.

When it was close to dusk, I went back to Candy's house, once again carrying the bunny in my mouth, hoping she'd be there with the others. When I saw her, however, she was alone. She'd been home for hours savoring her role in the daring rescue of the other rabbits whom, she assured me, were long gone — and on their way to establishing new lives.

Instead of being happy for the others, I was upset that my charge, br (short for small bunny rabbit), was now totally alone. I didn't have the heart to abandon him — to release him into the wild all by himself, so I decided to take br home with me. I knew that becoming involved with br's basic needs (like food and shelter) was an open invitation to him to step all over my boundaries, but it seemed the only sensible thing to do. As I said goodbye to Candy and picked up br to carry him home, I thought: "He's not heavy; he's my brother."

The trip was both mentally and physically exhausting. Unused to being carried by the scruff of the neck, br kept kicking his hind legs which made my burden even heavier. The entire time, my mind raced in high gear about the reception we'd receive. I was far from certain that the others would welcome a rabbit into our midst, particularly The Won, who was still indifferent to all living things, including us.

Exhausted, I finally had to put br down on the sidewalk, asking him to "hop along after me." (Wasn't there a famous cowboy by that name?) I knew he'd probably never been out of a cage before and that he had every right to be afraid, so I started telling him all the advantages of freedom. The ungrateful little twit had the nerve to tell me that freedom wasn't as much a state of being as it was a state of mind — making conscious choices and accepting their consequences without blame, shame or guilt. I was losing patience fast, and asked him if he'd literally rather be in a stew, which made him cry. I couldn't seem to stop his tears, so I tried a different tact and reassured him. "It's OK to cry. Actually, the more you cry, the less you'll have to pee," I said, forgetting where I'd picked up that particular piece of medical intelligence.

I told him to try not to think about the whole journey. If he just followed me, one hop at a time, we'd be home before we knew it, but it was dark by the time we arrived at my cat door. (What a grueling, stressful day!) I showed br how to lower his head and brush the flap open— twice — but his ears kept getting in the way. He used them as antennae, just like cats use their whiskers to judge whether or not they can clear a space. When br wouldn't budge, I finally lost patience with him and shoved him in front of me through the door. Thus, br arrived at The Won's the same way I'd made my grand entrance — feet first, being pushed from behind — a breech birth, so to speak.

88

Almost immediately br was surrounded by the curious trio of Angus, Billy and Bobby. I'd never realized how much Angus resembled a rabbit — except for his size and the length of his ears and tail. br noticed the similarity, too, and immediately bonded with Angus. "Don't crowd the little guy," I cautioned my brothers who watched with interest as br first hopped over to Angus, laying underneath the dining room table, then to the table itself, where he contentedly gnawed on its wooden legs.

Nathan came down the stairs looking like an unmade bed. He'd just awakened from a deep sleep and kept blinking, unable to believe his eyes when he saw br.

I explained the day's events and my decision to bring br home. My story was forthright and to the point which was a bit unlike me. Usually no facts were involved in any of my explanations. "I wasn't wrong to bring him home, was I?"

Nathan confirmed that I'd done the right thing. "Now let's decide how to best introduce br to The Won," he said, admitting he didn't have all the answers. I loved Nathan's humility; he was the only creature I knew who regularly undertook a realistic appraisal of himself.

We agreed that br should stay in the large walk-in closet where the kitty litter pan was kept, so he could be out of sight and toilet trained at the same time. The Won would take a much kinder view of an additional pet if that pet was already housebroken, we suspected. Heck, if we remained sufficiently nonchalant about br, by the time The Won discovered him, he might not even notice br was a rabbit.

It had been an exhausting but fulfilling day. I felt like I was finally giving back some of the kindness that had been extended to me. I knew I'd sleep well because Nathan always said: "Takers may eat better, but givers sleep better."

Fred and little br.

Chapter Eleven
The Newest Newcomer

For the next few days, br resided in the "litter" closet, but he was so darned cute, he was never alone in there for very long. Angus spent the most time with br, curling up so close to him you couldn't tell where one ended and the other began. Angus always did have an affinity for other creatures to whom he talked nonstop, but in br's case, Angus exercised restraint of tongue for once and didn't overwhelm br by talking his economy-sized ears off. Bill and Bob also visited the rabbit out of curiosity, but seldom stayed long, while Nathan stopped in at least once a day to ask br how he was doing and offer words of encouragement. Between all this coming and going, I was hard-pressed to find time alone with br for whom I felt responsible. After all, I'd saved his life. At the time, I couldn't see that I had the same "ownership" issue with br as Bobby'd had with me after he rescued me and brought me home.

To tell the truth, I was a little resentful of all the attention br was receiving. I liked being the focus of attention and couldn't get used to the fact that, all of a sudden, my light was hidden under a bushel — or in this case, behind a bunny. It was bad enough I'd surrendered my position as newcomer in the household, but now I was being forced to surrender my influence on br as well, since the others were edging me out. I couldn't understand why br preferred Angus' company to mine, when I was so much more interesting and better read. (I slept on the newspaper almost every day.) I knew I shouldn't be angry with br — it wasn't his fault he was so popular — but I was, which made me a tad insensitive.

On the third morning br was with us, I stopped in the closet to legitimately use the litter. br was alone for a change, nibbling on the food Bobby left for him. I did notice that br had used the litter for its intended purpose. "Smart Ass," I thought. I would have kicked sand in his face, but that would have been too blatantly hostile, so I settled on intimidation instead. I looked the small rabbit straight in the eye and said, "I don't know if anyone's mentioned this or not, br, but we're all very spiritual in this house." I said it in a tone that implied br wasn't welcome unless he, too, was spiritual (even though I felt like a hypocrite as soon as I said it.)

I certainly wasn't spiritual at br's age and didn't pretend to have a conscious contact with God. (My only contact with God was to pray for favors, then ignore Him if He didn't deliver.) But that was beside the point. I wasn't trying to be fair; I was trying to be mean and intimidating.

Little br looked up from his dish puzzled. He didn't seem to have a clue as to what I was talking about.

"So, do you have a God in your life?" I asked belligerently, hoping I was making him feel inferior.

His pink nose began to twitch out of control, a sign of agitation. Then he started to cry. Now that I'd achieved the desired result, I truly felt horrible. I suffered that sinking sensation in the pit of my stomach that signaled I wasn't living up to my own values — spiritual indigestion.

I stuck my head out the door and looked around to make sure no one had heard me. I nearly had a heart attack when I saw Nathan standing on the other side of the door.

"Fred, you should be ashamed of yourself," he chastised me. "Now step out of there, please, and let me try to repair the damage you've done." Nathan said sternly.

If I'd been Indian, my name would have been "One-Who's-Tail-Hangs-Low-From-Shame." I knew I'd have to eventually make an amends to br, admitting that my jealousy over the attention he was receiving from the others had spawned a mean streak, which, incidentally, was totally out of character. I quickly got out of Nathan's way and started to leave, but my curiosity got the better of me. I wanted to hear if Nathan was going to say anything derogatory about me. When he started talking about himself and the original BR instead, I was relieved. "It really isn't always about me," I said surprised.

It was obvious Nathan was trying to rebuild br's self-esteem with tales about the little bunny's proud lineage. He spoke of BR, his own mentor, and BR's family, Brer Rabbit, Pere Rabbit, Mere Rabbit and Frere Rabbit. Nathan talked about BR's involuntary confinement, his unbroken spirit, his contentment and his wisdom. Nathan said he'd learned all about spirituality from BR and that he would teach the little rabbit what he'd been taught. He told br not to worry about having a God in his life right now — obviously a reference to what I'd said, as well as an effort to allay any fears br might have that we were some sort of cult.

Nathan assured br that he'd never be told what to believe. Rather, he'd receive some general lessons about life and the desirability of relying on a power greater than himself. Then, it would be up to br to interpret and use that information — or not. Nathan assured br that it was natural to feel a little lost right now, but, not to worry; he'd eventually find his place.

I didn't hear br utter a word while Nathan talked, but I could picture his ears flapping as he nodded his head in the affirmative. Then br started asking Nathan a whole series of questions about our customs and social mores, which left me stunned. There was much more to this cute, little bunny than there first appeared to be. It was plain to see that he had an inordinate thirst for knowledge and hunger for acceptance; he was also far more intelligent than I suspected. I was so intent on eavesdropping, I didn't notice The Won standing over me.

"Scoot, Fred," he said, holding a large green plastic bag.

"Oh, oh," I thought, "the jig is up!" I realized The Won was about to go into the closet to change our litter. I wanted to warn Nathan, but it was too late. The Won had already swung the door of the closet open, revealing Nathan hunkered down in front of br who was scratching his ear with his size 12 foot. They were both startled, but only Nathan maintained his aplomb while br hastily retreated behind the water heater like a scared rabbit.

The Won was surprised to say the least. "Good God, Nathan, what in the world have you trapped in the closet?" He naturally assumed the bunny had gotten into the house by mistake and Nathan had hunted him down.

Nathan continued sitting where he was, changing only the expression on his face — from one of surprise to one of aggression, something more suitable for a fierce hunter.

The Won dropped the green plastic bag and carefully reached behind the water heater, extracting little br by the ears. He then cuddled the bunny in the palm of his hand, gently

94

petting him while speaking in a soft, soothing voice. "I bet you're lost, little guy. You must be someone's Easter bunny." The Won said. "Don't be afraid; I won't let the cats hurt you."

"As if we would," I thought, watching this tender scene from a distance. We were hardly brutal killers — unless you counted flies. Nathan rubbed up against The Won's leg to show him that he bore no hostility toward the bunny, and The Won understood the gesture immediately. He and Nathan always did share a unique ability to communicate. They were much more than owner and pet; they'd been soulmates, born of loneliness and nurtured by unconditional love, since The Won selected Nathan from a basketful of kittens at Nathan's Bar in Georgetown more than eighteen years before.

When The Won lowered br to Nathan's level so the cat could smell him, Nathan pretended to introduce himself by brushing his head against the bunny in a universal gesture of friendship. I could see that The Won was pleased. He brought br down to the living room. "Now for the acid test," he said. "We'll see if the others are as friendly." Obviously, we were, especially Angus who was so excited that his friend had finally "come out of the closet," he nearly bowled him over.

I hung back. I'm sure The Won interpreted my reluctance to approach the rabbit as timidity, but it obviously wasn't. I was embarrassed over my earlier mean-spiritedness and knew I owed br an amends. I didn't want to have to make my amends in front of the entire family, but it looked like that's exactly what was about to happen. Talk about humility!

The next opportunity I was alone with br, I told him all about myself to demonstrate my vulnerability. I apologized

95

again for trying to intimidate him with my statement about spirituality and admitted that I hadn't known anything about it at his age. I told him I'd be happy to work with him, and handed him one of my cards which read: "For a Spiritual Time, Call 1-800- FRED."

Returning my card, br said he really didn't need my help, thank you very much. He had a "Hare Power" in his life and had only been confused by my reference to "God." He'd also been too polite to interrupt Nathan when the older cat offered to help br get in touch with his spirituality. br said he learned a long time ago that if you didn't believe in "God," there was no adequate explanation; however, if you did believe, none was necessary.

"Oh," was the only thing I could say. I'd just undergone an ego-rectomy and, even though I might have deserved it, I didn't like it one bit. It was everything I could do to be nice to this precocious brat. "Well, maybe I can help you with the house rules then," I offered, surprised that I actually meant it.

Little br hesitated. I knew how he felt. I hated other people's rules and only complied when disobedience became really irritating or painful. However, br finally agreed to let me help him and I felt good. I always felt good when I could say, "I work for God, and that's the deal."

It was fortuitous that I learned my lesson about jealousy where br was concerned, because he not only charmed the flanks off of Nathan and my siblings, he soon became a favorite of The Won's as well — although The Won would have denied it had anyone suggested such a thing.

96

The Won didn't seem the least bit apprehensive about integrating a rabbit into our household, but I was concerned about adding another warm body to The Won's already crowded bed, especially such a small body. I was afraid br would become lost or suffocate in the cloud of cat hair that arose from the bedspread every time one of us jumped on it. I needn't have worried, however, because br actually preferred sleeping elsewhere, all by himself — in a shoe box lined with a soft pillow that The Won set up for him in a corner of the bedroom. Now I had another resentment. It had never occurred to me to ask for my "own room."

None of us could have anticipated the effect little br would have on The Won. Goodbye depression and hello passion for life! I found it amazing that the same lessons that applied to cats also applied to humans — helping another always made you feel better about yourself. So as The Won helped br adjust to his new home, he fell in love with life again, and that love multiplied and overflowed to all of us.

I believe that God sent br to The Won. I loved being right, and this theory, of course, supported my original cure for The Won's depression — bringing him a new friend to replace those he'd lost. I hadn't been mistaken about the cure, I insisted to anyone who'd listen, only a little misguided about the medicine and who would provide it.

I also realized that br was the answer to my prayers, the "someone" to whom I could pass the knowledge that Nathan and Bobby had given me. Passing it on to my brother was part of the great continuum of life. Again, God had provided exactly what I needed when I needed it.

97

Sometimes I worried I didn't have Nathan's unique understanding of rabbits to be an effective teacher, but then I'd remember that BR didn't have a unique understanding of cats when he began working with Nathan. When I expressed my concern to Nathan, he said God wasn't worried about my ability or inability, only about my availability. Besides, Nathan volunteered to help me with br's education on an *ad hoc* basis. Nathan said it was only fitting since it would bring his life full circle. He'd learned everything about being happy from one rabbit and now he'd have a chance to pass on that same knowledge to another rabbit. Even I could see God's handiwork in this series of "coincidences."

Fred instructing br.

Chapter Twelve
Recovery and Discovery

As I sat on the landing to the living room, watching The Won do his back exercises on the floor, I was delighted he was back to being 100%. (Well, maybe 98% — he still had a small dark side to his personality — an irrational dislike for TV newscaster Peter Jennings at whom he'd snarl before switching to another station as the man appeared on camera.) The Won was definitely feeling better though, because he no longer wore his brown cardigan sweater and sweatpants every day, an outfit I called his basic pitifuls. He was also once again taking action to improve himself.

The good news was that he was concerned with his appearance; the bad news was that his appearance confirmed that, like Nathan, he was getting old. When he looked at himself critically, he saw thinning hair, a thickening waistline, blurred vision, teeth drifting apart, and horizontal lines across his forehead that looked as though he'd been resting it against the Venetian blinds. Where once The Won frequented new, hip joints; now he worried about having new hip joints. Where once he worried about who'd come to his parties, he now worried about who'd come to his funeral. Where once he tried to look like Brando, now he tried not to look like Brando. This was the head of our family — the human who put the "fun" in dysfunctional.

When The Won was in a positive frame of mind, he tried to neutralize the aging process by going to the gym at least three times a week, where he'd spend most of the day. The gym wasn't just a place to exercise; it was an "experience." He spent so many hours undressing, dressing, stretching, going for a sauna and steam, showering and appraising the fitness of others, he was usually hard-pressed to find time to actually exercise, but it didn't really matter. The Won got plenty of exercise at home. The latest project to keep him in shape was the construction of a multi-tiered cat condo for us that rivaled anything designed or built by Frank Lloyd Wright. The bottom tier had a special compartment for br, who couldn't climb to the higher platforms like the rest of us.

Another of The Won's hobbies was travel, but he hadn't gone anywhere since he took a winter vacation several years ago, leaving a friend in charge of the house and Nathan. The friend booted Nathan out the back door as soon as the sound of The Won's car faded in the distance, and kept Nathan locked out of the house for the full two weeks The Won was gone. It was the dead of winter and Nathan had to really hustle to survive. When The Won returned and found out what had happened, he felt so guilty, he'd never taken another vacation away from home since. However, this year was going to be different. We were all going to a rented house in Florida.

Being an adventurer, I thought it sounded very exciting. Personally, I was looking forward to new experiences with sand fleas, fire ants, "no-seeums" and alligators. Billy, a wet blanket when it came to anything new, kept asking *why* we had to go, which prompted a comment about acceptance from Nathan. "To question why is ego; to question how is spiritual." Quite frankly, I wasn't sure I wanted to know *how* we were all going to get to Florida, but it didn't matter. Nathan's admonition stanched the flow of questions that hemorrhaged from the rest of us about the trip.

Every day for a week, after instructing br in some of the more basic lessons of residential living, I watched The Won prepare for our trip. He called the newspaper to have delivery stopped, filled out forms to have his mail forwarded, paid bills two months in advance so we'd have utilities when we returned, did laundry, and packed the car with our supplies — clean pans of kitty litter, water dishes, food and blankets. By the time he was finished, we looked like refugees fleeing Kosovo with all our worldly belongings.

Finally the day arrived when it was time to leave. The car was truly a sight to behold. With all of our stuff inside it, including an emergency cat carrier in the trunk, the only place left for The Won's suitcases was on the roof, to which they were fastened by bungee cords threaded through the car's opened windows. The Won brought us down to the car one at a time, leaving Angus and br for last. The only time any of us had ever been in the car was en route to Dr. Gary's, so we equated automobiles with pain and fear, which we expressed in a cacophony of meowing as soon as the engine turned over.

I could see by the set of The Won's jaw and the clench of his teeth that he was irritated by the racket we were making. I'm sure he thought we'd either develop laryngitis or tire of our caterwauling by the time we reached I-95 South — but he was wrong on both counts. The Won wasn't the only passenger we were disturbing. Confused by our reaction to the automobile, br was sitting in the cup holder on the console between the front seats with his ears doubled over to muffle the noise.

Before putting us in the car, The Won gave us all tranquilizers at Dr. Gary's suggestion. Obviously, they hadn't begun to work yet. So as he drove off, The Won popped a couple into his own mouth. Then, inserting a classical tape into the tape deck, he turned up the music as loud as he could — to soothe the savage beasts — but the tape was no match for our arias.

I was the most composed, uttering only an occasional whimper, until we neared Fredericksburg, where Bobby got car sick and Nathan, who'd nervously been washing himself since we left, disgorged a record-setting furball. Billy and Angus continued screeching in harmony, adding tension to the already toxic environment. No longer immune to the chaos, I began to hyperventilate.

The Won was clearly at his wits end when a loud thump emanated from the roof. I looked back just in time to see one of the suitcases bounce off the back of the car and onto the highway, opening and spilling its contents of socks, tee shirts, jockey shorts and shoes. (I always wondered how a single shoe came to be lying along the side of a highway. Now I knew!)

"Oh shit," The Won muttered as the second bungee cord snapped. Only this time the suitcase opened before it fell off the roof. Shirts blew from the top of the car, catching on the windshield wipers and aerial. Quickly glancing in the rear view mirror, The Won slammed on the brakes and came to a screeching halt on the shoulder of the road. He got out of the car in a cloud of burned rubber to view the devastation behind him. The only positive thing I could say about the entire incident was that it shocked us all into silence.

After gathering a few of his belongings from the roadside, The Won announced that our vacation was officially over. I think I was the only one who was disappointed. The

103

return journey was a quiet one. The tranquilizers we'd been given had finally kicked in and we slept all the way home — except br, who was still sitting wide-eyed in the cup holder.

I consoled myself that, once again home, I could concentrate in earnest on br's lessons without any further distractions. He was a quick study and I loved teaching him. It wasn't a matter of recognition either. Doing good felt good.

About a week after our return from our aborted vacation, I couldn't find br downstairs, so I went into The Won's bedroom. It was unlike br to be in his shoe box during the day, which is where I found him curled into a tight little ball. I ran downstairs to get The Won and, like Lassie, finally convinced him to follow me up to the bedroom, though it was done in fits and starts. (I wondered how Lassie made his owner follow him for miles on much more complicated itineraries with only one or two barks.) The Won knew br was sick as soon as he saw him, so br's second ride in an automobile validated all of our experiences. It was fear and pain-based — to Dr. Gary's.

Little br had to stay at the vet for observation overnight, which made me realize how much I missed the little guy when he wasn't around. I felt as close to him as I did to Nathan and Bobby, who'd also become ill with a mysterious virus, giving me the opportunity to deliver kibbles to him just as he'd delivered them to me so long ago.

When The Won brought br home, it was clear from his drooping ears that the little rabbit needed to rest for a few days. I felt sorry for my brave, smart, little brother, and I was impatient to spend time with him, but I knew I'd have to wait until he was feeling better. Temporarily freed from my teaching duties, I followed The Won around while he hunted and gathered tools, pieces of wood, and wire mesh. When it was clear he was constructing an outdoor cage on the deck, I panicked. Fear sliced through my heart like a dagger. I was convinced The Won was going to keep us all confined to the house or a cage from now on — an overreaction to br and Bobby both getting sick. I was sure The Won thought we'd all be much safer if we were kept in captivity. I knew The Won wasn't going to let us outside anymore, just as I knew I couldn't possibly remain here under those conditions.

I needed freedom and excitement. I didn't want to be like the old man in the nursing home who sat in the corner crying all the time. When one of the attendants approached the old man to ease his fears, he asked, "Why are you crying? Are you afraid to die?" "No, no," the old man replied. "I'm not afraid to die. I'm crying because I was afraid to live." I'd never been afraid to live, and I knew I'd be miserable if I had to restrict my life because of someone else's fears.

I naturally projected that's exactly what was going to happen and I'd once again be forced to leave home. I dredged up every bad feeling I'd ever had about leaving my mother and sisters, wallowing in what I considered my abandonment issue. I was devastated that I'd have to leave my family behind, particularly little br, but I'd already mentally packed my knapsack, loaded it on my back, and was heading out the door. I would run away to Candy's where at least I'd have my freedom. On second thought, I'd go to my sisters'; it was nicer.

"What are you thinking about?" Bobby asked, noticing my scowl and interrupting my projecting.

"That cage The Won is building for us. Aren't you worried?" I asked over The Won's hammering.

"Not particularly," Bobby said. "I know what it's for."

It was clear Bobby wasn't going to volunteer the information and that he wanted me to pry it out of him. I was sure I already knew, so Bobby's explanation came as a complete surprise.

"The cage is so br can go outside." Bobby commented nonchalantly.

"Why does br need to be in a cage when he's outside?" I asked puzzled. The only wildlife in the neighborhood are a few wild rabbits — he's in no danger," I observed.

Bobby watched my reaction as he said, "The Won wants br caged because he's afraid SHE'LL get pregnant."

I fainted!

Chapter Thirteen
Nathan's Spiritual Legacy

I couldn't get used to the fact that br was a girl. Sure, her soprano voice should have been a dead giveaway, but I thought that was due to youth. I assumed br's voice hadn't changed yet because "he" was still so small — no bigger than a teacup. Once br's sex was revealed, her high-pitched voice made perfect sense, but not her inordinately small size about which I was still curious.

I didn't want to risk offending her, so I asked Nathan if she was "normal" or whether she was a midget rabbit. ("Short hare" may have been more politically correct, but I hesitated using a term that had a negative connotation for cats since it described the most common breed, which, incidentally, included Nathan, Billy, Bobby and me.) Nathan applauded my sensitivity, but told me br's size was genetically engineered; she was actually a mature cup bunny, bred to be tiny and easily handled by magicians performing magic tricks.

With her squinting eyes and slightly bucked teeth, I couldn't picture br in show business, but, come to think of it, she wasn't in show business, was she? I wondered if, like cats, rabbits had a caste system and where cup bunnies fell within it, but decided it was none of my business. Dealing with br's gender was worrisome enough without tackling her entire gene pool.

Who was I kidding? All of my musings about br were merely diversionary tactics employed to skirt the real issue —

my willingness to teach a girl. "What to do, what to do, what to do?" I pondered. I prided myself on being a liberal. I certainly wasn't a racist, nor did I consider myself a sexist tom, the feline version of a male chauvinist pig. However, I did admit to having misgivings about being able to treat br like merely another student, "one of the boys" so to speak.

Then I had a most intriguing thought. I remembered one of Bobby's early admonitions when I'd sought out attractive young females to mentor. Bobby, who recognized my motives for what they were, cautioned that it was best for toms to teach other toms while females taught other females. Mentally smiling, I looked for Nathan to confirm this unwritten rule, but Nathan threw me a curve. He assured me the rule didn't pertain to cross-species situations, so if I were looking for an excuse to shirk my duties, this wouldn't be it. (It was as though Nathan could read my mind, a talent I envied. I definitely wasn't a mind reader; I was barely a mind user.)

I thought I'd done a pretty good job of hiding my emotional confusion from br by busily washing myself whenever she approached. By avoiding eye contact with her, I didn't think she realized how uncomfortable I'd become around her. Then, passing me in the hall one morning, she raised her tiny paw in front of her slightly crossed eyes and shook it at me while mouthing the words "girl power" as she hopped by. She looked so silly, we both started laughing, which broke the ice and melted away any reservations I may have had about being her teacher. Our souls had touched through laughter and I knew everything was going to be all right.

Working with br wouldn't be easy because she was almost too smart for her own good. Nathan always said he'd never seen anyone too dumb to learn, but he'd seen a lot of creatures who were too smart to learn. So I did ask br to promise me that she wouldn't intellectualize everything I said, be true to her emotions and do her best to follow my directions. "What an order, I can't go through with it!" was her initial response before conceding that she'd try to do her best. (I had good reason to be suspicious of the word "try.")

I usually conducted br's lessons outside, sitting in front of her cage, so I was glad The Won had built a raised platform in it that allowed us to be at eye level. It was much easier to intimidate br eye-to-eye when she insisted on doing things her way or paid less than rapt attention to her lessons. Once in awhile I'd catch her flirting with the brown and white wild rabbit who lounged around the yard, admiring br from a distance. Nathan had forewarned me that most female rabbits had sex issues — pat their heads and their pants fell off. Despite his warning, I was going to let this lounge lizard visit br, just so she could have some contact with one of her own kind. However, in the end, fear overrode my sentimentality.

I suspected the "wild" rabbit was named after his behavior rather than his environment. Truthfully, I was terrified that, like the aliens in "B" movies, br would breed baby bunnies so fast, we cats would soon find ourselves vastly outnumbered — an inferior species serving our new rabbit masters. When all was said and done, I was glad I practiced, "When in doubt, nothing is often the best thing to do and nothing is always the best thing to say" because the situation resolved itself. The brown and white hare finally left and a couple of female bunnies eventually appeared, who now visited br on a regular basis.

I was fortunate that Nathan was willing to substitute teach for me when I was occasionally too burned out to continue. Sometimes I could stretch my patience by using the "Just Like Me" exercise he'd taught me. He said the things about br that bothered me the most were probably the same things I disliked most about myself. So I'd recite, "Just like me, br is a know-it-all; just like me, br refuses to follow directions; just like me, br is disrespectful; just like me, br would rather get attention than give it"... Nathan assured me that if I persevered with br's lessons, one day I'd be able to say, "just like me, br is happily and usefully whole."

Nathan recognized that cats needed encouragement every once in awhile and he was always first in line to scratch my back. But nothing meant more to me than when he put me in the same category as himself and talked about "our" joy in helping others. He'd recite:

> " I have wept in the night
> For the shortness of sight
> That to somebody's need made me blind,
> But I have never yet
> Felt a tinge of regret
> For being a little too kind."

Sometimes I found it hard to believe how deeply I could be touched by his words — me, a street tough, who's motto had been "Never Let Them See You Shed!" I was so grateful to The Won for giving me a home and to Nathan and Bobby for giving me a new perspective on life. They taught me how to be kind — by example. The one time I questioned why they were so considerate, they'd replied that it didn't take any longer to be kind than to be curt.

110

By the end of June, it was too hot for br to be in her cage on the deck, which received direct sunlight most of the day. So br's formal lessons were suspended for the summer. I thought this was an original idea until Bobby mentioned the words "summer vacation," which had a familiar ring.

I was glad for the teaching hiatus so I could spend more time dancing with Ginger (yes, I was seeing her again, only this time on a platonic basis), visiting my mother and sisters, and playing with members of my immediate family. All work and no play made Fred a "cat-astrophe." It had been a long time since I'd hunted flies with Billy and Bobby, played practical jokes on Angus, followed The Won around the yard as he planted grass seed in ground where grass was never meant to grow, and sunned on the deck with Nathan. I learned a long time ago that I needed this kind of balance in my life.

Nathan believed in having a special place where he could commune with his Higher Meower, and that special place was our deck in the early morning as the sun rose over the azalea bushes. So I never disturbed him there until well into mid-morning. As I seated myself next to him, my white paws crossed and hanging over the edge of the deck, I kept quiet, enjoying the buzzing of the bees, the chirping of the birds, and the chattering of the squirrels, until Nathan finally spoke.

Nathan loved to talk. He said the secret to a fulfilling life was simply "one cat talking to another cat." He liked to reminisce about his destiny, which he said was as much a matter of choice as chance. He wondered what his life would be like today if he'd gotten what he wanted when he was a kitten — which was to be left alone under the dark, dreary porch where he was born. He wasn't the only one who

111

wondered about such things. Ex-President Reagan apparently had a similar thought when he was writing his autobiography and penned, "If I'd gotten that job I wanted at Montgomery Ward, I suppose I never would have left Illinois."

Nathan attributed his forced eviction and adoption by The Won as "chance," but said his relationship with BR, which led to his emotional growth, was definitely a matter of choice. Being run over by The Won was "chance," but seeking and finding a loving Higher Meower as a result of the accident was choice. Losing BR was "chance," but passing on to Bobby what BR taught him was choice. Then temporarily losing his faith was choice, but my entry into his life which ultimately restored his faith was "chance."

Nathan said when he substituted "God's will" for "chance," it was clear how God had guided his life. He admitted that his understanding of God's will, which he called "The Vision," was only possible in hindsight. Nathan said I, too, might eventually be rewarded with my own vision of how God worked in my life, but the way to insure it was to continue to work with others.

Nathan believed that God's intention was for us to love and help others like He loved and helped us. That's why it was called God's work. If God did it all Himself, we'd be the ones to suffer because we wouldn't need each other and we'd be very lonely, disconnected creatures. He said that my relationship with br would take my spirituality to new heights, and that I'd surely meet others as I trudged the road to happy destiny. Nathan assured me that leading a spiritual life was a joyful journey. He told me not to be confused by the word "trudge;" it simply meant "to walk with purpose."

Insofar as our relationship with man was concerned, Nathan said cats had forged that bond millions of years ago with man's earliest ancestors. Cats always had an affinity for man, but human scientists only recently became aware of the primitive origins of that relationship when Cocoa the Gorilla adopted Smoky the Kitten and the "news" made world headlines. Nathan commented that we cats had certainly evolved well and "man" hadn't done too badly either, although he'd lost a lot of hair.

Nathan said he was spending more time at the top of our hill visiting the Clarke Cat Cemetery where all our predecessors were buried in Samsonite suitcases. He said he went there frequently to thank his Higher Meower for each of us. He admitted that he rarely visited BR's grave anymore because it was too far away, but BR was always in his thoughts and very much alive in Bobby and me. Nathan choked up when he told me how proud BR would be to see me sitting in front of little br's cage, teaching her what BR had originally taught him.

Composing himself again, Nathan called my journey his spiritual legacy. He truly felt that his life had been a life well led and he promised me that if I continued doing what I was doing, I'd be able to say the same when I was his age. I already considered myself a vision seeker, but I didn't need to tell Nathan that. A sign of my personal growth was letting Nathan have the last word.

Nathan's Epilogue

Sitting on the deck with The Won, he in his polka-dot shirt and me in my stripes, both chewing a piece of grass while watching the sun slowly rise over the azaleas on the hill, I am savoring life and concentrating on my breathing, a meditation technique BR taught me. Normally, The Won isn't up this early unless he can't sleep, like this morning. I don't know what he's thinking about as we sit here quietly, but I know what I'm thinking about — my incredible life — and what I'm feeling — inordinate gratitude for it.

When The Won first brought me home nearly eighteen years ago, I was so self-reliant and suspicious, I resisted everything he tried to do for me. I didn't have a clue about who I was or what I felt — except uncomfortable. I was raw and edgy, like I was wearing my fur inside out, and I worried about everything. I didn't know that 99% of the things I worried about would never happen, and that the things I had reason to worry about would happen so unexpectedly, I'd never have a chance to worry about them before they happened.

My basic problem was lack of trust until I learned to trust The Won, which was a result of my experience with him. Once I crossed that threshold, it became less difficult to trust others, particularly BR who led me on my spiritual journey. (Gosh, how I miss BR. He did more good by accident than most creatures do on purpose.)

The next step was to trust God, which also proved to be a result of my experience with Him. I discovered that trusting God with my life was its own reward because it gave me an

114

incredible feeling that things were exactly as they should be at any particular moment in time, that everything *would* be all right, and that I was never alone.

I am always amazed at the imaginative ways God has met me at the level of my needs and taken care of me over the years. He's always exceeded my expectations of myself as long as I kept the lines of communication open to Him through prayer. (Personally, I find dawn the perfect time to commune with my God, before He is distracted by the 45 million requests for new jobs, the 33 million petitions for a "relationship," the 106 million prayers for financial stability, and the countless millions of other requests that divert His attention from me.)

BR, who served as my example of an avid proponent and practitioner of prayer, was also very practical, insisting that what I said and did on my feet was as important as what I said and did on my knees. He told me it wasn't enough to think noble thoughts; I had to follow them through with noble deeds. I sometimes still surprise myself when I commit a random act of kindness because it is such a far cry from the self-absorbed, cynical little twit that I used to be, always seeing the glass half empty instead of half full.

I find it ironic that what I treasure most today — the relationship I have with my Higher Meower and my fellows — is something I never knew I wanted until I was exposed to BR's way of life. When I was a doubting tom, BR asked me to suspend my disbelief long enough for my spirit to grow. He knew that if I stayed open-minded and improved my character by following his suggestions, I wouldn't need to worry about finding God; God would find me. I would be contacted — and indeed I was.

At first it was hard being a spiritual giant in an imperfect world, until BR taught me about acceptance. He said acceptance was recognizing that no matter how much was in the glass, the glass was as full as it was going to get at that moment. BR said that life wasn't always fair and I needed to learn the difference between acceptance and approval. I needed to learn to accept the things I couldn't change, and change the things I could. He said my challenge was to continue to grow along spiritual lines and to try to make a difference in the world. BR taught me that if I didn't like what I saw out there, I needed to be what I wanted to see, I needed to say what I wanted to hear, I needed to do what had to be done. BR told me that if I was the best Nathan I could be, I'd achieve peace of mind and feel happily and usefully whole — and he was right, as usual.

The faint sound of Fred and br's voices, drifting from the open window in the den, interrupted my reverie.

"How long do I have to take these 'life' lessons, Fred?" br was asking impatiently.

Fred laughed. "When I asked Nathan the same question, he said 'until I liked them,'" Fred replied. "Now, I know you're much smarter than that, so why don't you just tell me how happy you want to be, and I'll adjust the schedule accordingly."

I smiled. Fred was the third generation to pass on this process of self-awareness, self-forgiving and self-forgetting — a process that leads to fully trusting God. He'd learned that instead of asking God for what he thought he wanted, he should ask God to show him what was in store for him, then pray for guidance to develop the qualities necessary to make God's vision for him a reality. Compared to the rest of us, little br had a head start on spirituality because she already believed in a loving God whom she made her co-pilot. So now all Fred and I have to do is convince her to switch seats with Him. When br puts her Hare Power in the pilot's seat and surrenders the illusion of control, she'll gain a new perspective on the circumstances of her life and know peace of mind (God's nod of approval) regardless of what those circumstances happen to be. Then she'll discover that God really does bestow the greatest gifts on those who let Him choose.

I love the way The Won strokes my back. My heart is full and I am grateful for everything I've ever been given, especially grace and mercy. Through grace I got many things I didn't deserve, and through mercy I didn't get some of the things I did deserve before I learned how to be a better version of myself. I finally feel whole — capable of giving and receiving unconditional love — tending the sheep, while my Higher Meower tends me. If the most valuable thing I own today is how I feel, I can honestly say I am rich beyond measure.

As long as I continue to do what I've been doing — trust God, keep my own house in order, and help others — I'll live "happily ever after," because BR taught me that happiness is a by-product of right living.

Nathan — October, 1999

PRECEDING BOOKS IN THE NATHAN TRILOGY

NATHAN...The Spiritual Journey of an Uncommon Cat
By Jacqueline Clarke

This first book, published in 1998, begins the Nathan trilogy, humorous, light-hearted, adult parables. *NATHAN* is about the spiritual and psychological growth of a troubled but teachable tomcat who learns everything he needs to know about living life on life's terms from his mentor, a rabbit, incarcerated across the street for sex offenses.

Nathan's account of finding happiness and serenity while overcoming jealousy, fear, insecurity, humiliation and grief is filled with valuable life lessons, like:

> Happiness isn't having what you want, but wanting what you have.

> You wouldn't care so much what others thought of you, if you realized how seldom they did.

> Religion consists of rules and rituals made by others to honor God, while spirituality is your own expression of love for God. It's about being useful and whole, not holy, and only involves one rule...The Golden Rule.

During his journey from self-centeredness to spirituality, Nathan evolves from one who occasionally acts kind to one who is kind — a creature of God who's found peace and contentment.

PRECEDING BOOKS IN THE NATHAN TRILOGY

Nathan, Spiritual Advisor to BILL and BOB
By Jacqueline Clarke

In this second book of the Nathan Trilogy, The Won adopts two new kittens to whom Nathan becomes a mentor. Laugh your way to emotional good health as these uncommon cats deal with family dynamics, relationships, surviving the Christmas holidays, and Nathan's temporary loss of faith. In this highly nutritional, easily-digestible supplement for the soul Nathan passes on lessons like:

Failure isn't falling down; it's refusing to get up again.

When you're going through Hell, keep moving.

Meaningful self-improvement for the long term is seldom accomplished in the short term.

Who we are is God's gift to us; what we become is our gift to Him.

When you're fearful, look for your shadow because God is the spirit and light within you.

A fast and funny read, *BILL and BOB* documents Bob's personality conversion (spiritual awakening). The message in *BILL and BOB* lies in its final chapter in which Nathan explains the ultimate secret to a happy life — The Vision.

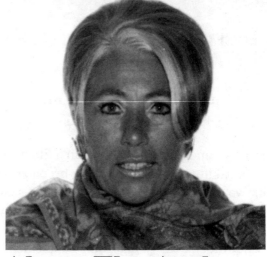

About The Author

Jacqueline Clarke has spent most of her career in the travel industry, first directing the development of advertising campaigns and sales promotional material for the U.S. Government's now defunct national tourist office, then as Vice President of Travel Programs for ENCORE, an international travel club, where she was also editor of their bi-monthly travel magazine.

Jackie's most important achievement to date, however, has been learning to lead a spiritual life on a day-to-day basis and appreciating her Higher Power's imagination and sense of humor. The Nathan Trilogy, funny adult parables about troubled tomcats who become happily and usefully whole through right living and spiritual growth, is a testament to what she's learned.

Jackie lives in the suburbs of Washington, D.C. with her two feline roommates, Bill and Bob.

GIVE THE GIFT OF LAUGHTER

ORDER FORM FOR MORE BOOKS

For **personally-autographed copies** of any of the books in the Nathan Trilogy, just send a check, cash, or money order for the total amount of the book(s), plus $3.50 for postage and handling for up to a combination of five books. For more than five books, send $5.00 for postage and handling.

Please send me _____ copies of NATHAN...
The Spiritual Journey of an Uncommon Cat
@ $7.99 each $_____

Please send me _____ copies of Nathan, Spiritual
Advisor to BILL and BOB @ $9.99 each $_____

Please send me _____ copies of Nathan's Spiritual
Legacy, FRED @ $9.99 each $_____

                              Postage - $3.50 or $5.00 $_____

                                     Total Enclosed $_____
Please autograph the book(s) to**: (Names)**

Tear out this page and send it to: Matou Communications, 3153-M Anchorway Court, Falls Church, VA 22042 with your check, money order or cash. 703 207-3574 (phone and fax)

Any of the books in the Nathan Trilogy can be ordered from any bookstore (or on the Internet at www.southbaybooks.com or www.amazon.com) by full title and author's name, Jacqueline Clarke, or by calling toll-free 1-888-5books5.